BRIDGER

BRIDGER

JAMES PATRICK HUNT

THORNDIKE PRESS
A part of Gale, Cengage Learning

GALE
CENGAGE Learning™

Detroit • New York • San Francisco • New Haven, Conn • Waterville, Maine • London

GALE
CENGAGE Learning™

LIBRARY OF CONGRESS CATALOGING-IN-PUBLICATION DATA

Hunt, James Patrick, 1964–
    Bridger / by James Patrick Hunt.
        p. cm. — (Thorndike Press large print mystery.)
    ISBN-13: 978-1-4104-3136-3 (hardcover)
    ISBN-10: 1-4104-3136-3 (hardcover)
    1. Thieves—Fiction. 2. Judges—Crimes against—Fiction. 3. Mafia—Fiction. 4. Large type books. I. Title.
    PS3608.U577B75 2010b
    813'.6—dc22   2010027400

Published in 2010 by arrangement with Tekno Books and Ed Gorman.

Printed in the United States of America
1 2 3 4 5 6 7 14 13 12 11 10

BRIDGER

ONE

It was late and there were only a few people on the train. Kids coming home from a night of clubbing in Manhattan. A young lady attorney who had worked late at a blue chip law firm on Wall Street and was beginning to wonder if the first year's salary was worth feeling like a serf. A fifty-year-old man contemplating disappointment in his career and fearing a merger at the bank and a concomitant layoff. Another guy with a shaved head had stayed late in the city so he could go to a whorehouse in Chinatown; he hoped his wife would be asleep when he got home so he could take a shower to wash off the smell. A cross-section of Westchester and other parts north, strangers to each other, keeping their thoughts to themselves. Vanity, insecurity, boredom and fear.

The train rolled under a street — a brief tunnel — and the volume created by the sound of wheels on tracks increased and echoed off walls for a couple of seconds, returned to normal when the train came out the other side.

Also on the train in that same car was a man of about forty. His hair was cut short and graying at the temples. He wore a black suit and black shoes with rubber soles. A quick glance at him and the black attaché case at his side might suggest that he was a lawyer or a business executive. He sat with his legs crossed, his hands folded across his lap. But look closer at the hands. Look closer and you see that, though clean, they are not soft. Strong and calloused and sure, the hands of a mechanic or a craftsman. His name was Dan Bridger.

Bridger got off the train in North Westchester. He looked at his watch. A few minutes past one A.M.

He stood for a few moments on the station platform, the sound of the train continuing north, then fading away. He was alone.

There were no cars in the parking lot.

He walked a mile, and then another half-mile, keeping out of lights and in shadows. When he reached the neurosurgeon's house, it was almost two o'clock in the morning. It was a sprawling mansion with white brick and brown faux-shutters and a brown roof.

A sally-port separating the servants' quarters from the main house, providing an entrance to the five-car garage behind. The grounds were expansive, grass rolling up like a well-kept carpet to the house. Trees and shrubs close to the brick wall surrounding the estate.

Bridger had seen it before in daylight, seven weeks earlier when he had been planning the job. He had taken photographs. He had memorized routes and schedules of the neighborhood security patrols. The white Chevrolet Impalas with white paint and blue stripes and cherry flashers on the top. Not bona-fide police officers driving them, but they were armed and, like most rent-a-cops, a little anxious to kill somebody.

Bridger crouched behind a clump of bushes across the street from the house. He remained still while one of the blue and white Impalas drove by.

When it was gone, he crossed the street and put himself in a dark spot next to the wall surrounding the neurosurgeon's house.

He opened the attaché case. Inside were his tools. Among the tools were three guns: a Glock .45 semi-automatic, a Smith and Wesson .38 snubnose, and a long-barreled tranquilizer gun. He took the tranquilizer gun out of the case and set it on the ground.

Then he took out a black rope and tied one end of it to the attaché case and the other around his ankle. He picked up the tranquilizer gun and put it in his jacket pocket. He jumped up and gripped the top of the brick wall and heaved himself up. He had just straddled the top when he heard the movement of the dog. A German shepherd, the growl coming now from deep in the dog's chest. As the dog approached, Bridger stilled himself and let it get closer. He fixed on the black and tan shape in the darkness, then raised the tranquilizer gun and fired. The dog made no sound when it fell to the ground.

Bridger waited.

Two, he thought. *There were two dogs here seven weeks ago.*

Shit.

Things could change in seven weeks. The second dog could have died, or been given away. Bridger reminded himself that dogs, generally, did not operate in stealth. Wolves, maybe. Wildcats, certainly. But a German shepherd would let you know its intention.

Bridger looked out into the darkness. He whistled.

The second dog came out and then into view. Confused and apprehensive, but growling now as well. Bridger shot that one too.

Using the rope, Bridger pulled the case up. He lowered it onto the grounds of the estate, then jumped down. He walked past the sleeping dogs — they would be out for six hours — and approached the house.

It was early spring, and there was dew on the grass. That meant that his steps would leave impressions. Normally, this would disturb him. But there was a brick wall separating the lawn from the street, so a patrol car would not be able to shine a spotlight on the grass and see the impressions.

The Chinaman — whose actual name had been Sam Chu-Lin — used to say that you shouldn't leave footprints. He would say that if the grass was wet, you should lie down and roll across it. He said a good patrolman might spot the tracks and stop and investigate. Sam had a lot of rules like that. Often, he was right. But Bridger hadn't accepted everything he said as gospel. For example, Sam had said that most dogs were friendly and would approach you gently if you snapped your fingers and said, "Hey, boy." Total nonsense. The first time Bridger had tried that, a twenty-pound poodle had left punctures deep enough in his hand to

11

require stitches, proving that you can give the little fellah a cute haircut but you weren't going to take all the wolf out of him. It was that incident that moved Bridger to add the tranquilizer gun to his retinue.

When he was nearer to the house, he removed a pair of black gloves and a black ski mask from the case and put them on. He edged around the house until he found the kitchen windows. That's where the telephone wires were. Bridger cut the line with a pair of wire cutters. Then he went to the back door that led into the kitchen. From the case he removed a pair of 16-inch pliers. He placed them on the doorknob and turned. Slow, but sure. It did not make much noise. He turned and then the lock was broken.

And he was in.

He took the tools he needed from the case, including the guns, and then put the case in the cabinet beneath the sink. He remained in the kitchen for a few moments, letting his eyes adjust to the interior darkness.

It was a big house. Big enough to function as a small museum. Bridger went through it, turning on a penlight. He went through the ground floor and unlocked every door he could find. Like any professional burglar, he wanted as many exits as possible.

Yet, when he got to the front door, he found that it was already unlocked.

Hmmm.

This in itself was not unusual. Even the wealthiest people could get careless. Still, it gave Bridger an uneasy feeling. The worst thing was to be in the middle of a burglary when the owners came home. Was everybody home?

The owner: Richard M. Kloberg, M.D., neurosurgeon, co-owner of a clinic in Manhattan. He had a couple of patents to his name and, combined with the income from his practice, he had become a very rich man. Married for the second time, two years ago, to the former Janet Heinlen, a woman about twenty-five years his junior. The former Mrs. Heinlen had a taste for jewelry.

Bridger walked down the hallway and when he got closer to the study, he heard voices murmuring . . . not conversing exactly, but making noises while the lights were off.

Bridger moved nearer to the doorway of the study, his penlight at his side — switched off. The door was closed. Bridger stood still and listened.

Man.

Two people making love. A woman and a

man who did not sound like he was sixty-three, the age of Richard M. Kloberg, M.D.

Bridger left them alone and moved upstairs. He found Kloberg asleep in the master bedroom. Alone. Bridger figured the woman downstairs was probably his wife. Sinners.

Bridger crept closer to the bed. He checked the nightstand for a weapon and didn't find one. Then he checked under the pillow. None there either.

Bridger took the .45 out of his pocket and turned on the bedside lamp. The glare of the light illuminated the old man's complexion, the liver spots in his skin. It made Bridger think of the people downstairs, for some reason.

Bridger shook him awake.

The doctor opened his eyes and Bridger said, "Hey."

Bridger knew enough about human nature to understand that the sight of someone in a black ski mask in the middle of the night will do something to a man. Terrorists, murderers, assassins — it's rarely good to see a ski mask. This immediate fear was useful, but you didn't want the person to become hysterical. They had to be calm enough to comply with demands.

Bridger said, "Relax. I'm only here to rob you."

"Oh, God. Oh, God," Kloberg said. "Don't kill me."

"Whether or not you're killed is strictly up to you," Bridger said. "Your wife's jewelry, where is it?"

The man hesitated. *Christ,* Bridger thought, sighed and pointed the .45 at the man's face. "What are you doing? You're insured."

"I —"

"So what do you want to mess around for?"

"I — I don't think it's all insured."

Lightly, Bridger rapped the barrel of the .45 on the man's knee. It was not enough to hurt him, but enough to send the message that things could get physical if he didn't cooperate. Usually the hint of violence was enough.

"Okay," the old man said, "okay. Over there in the top drawer in the dresser. The top drawer."

Bridger said, "Keep your hands on top of the blanket." He walked over and opened the drawer. Three pairs of diamond earrings and a string of pearls. He put the diamonds in his jacket pocket, left the pearls where they were.

Bridger looked at the man. He said, "Where's your wife?" Though he felt he knew the answer already, he wanted to know what the man thought.

Kloberg said, "She's at a fundraiser."

"When do you expect her back?"

"I don't know. If it gets too late, she stays in the city with a friend." The old man straightened in his bed. "What business is it of yours?"

None, Bridger thought. He said, "You've got a safe downstairs in your study. Tell me the combination."

Kloberg looked at him for a few moments. Small of stature and not getting any younger, but there was a resilience to him. He said, "You know about those stones, huh?"

Bridger suppressed a smile. Stones. The old fellah had seen too many movies.

"Yeah," Bridger said, "I know about them. Tell me the combination, I'll tie you up and be on my way."

The man actually shook his head.

He said, "I can do that, but you'll mess it up and come back up here and untie me and then we'll both have to go down there. If you don't mind, I'd just as soon be done with this as soon as possible."

"Just tell me the combination."

16

"It's hinky. I'm going to have to do it. Look," the old man said, "I don't have a gun in there. It's just money. I have no reason to try anything. I'm sixty years old and I've got nothing left to prove. It's a hinky lock and I need to open it for you. That's all."

Bridger let a few moments pass.

Then said, "You've got a point." He picked up the man's bathrobe off a chair and handed it to him. "But I don't think you're going to be happy."

Five minutes later, Bridger had a domestic situation on his hands. His suspicion had been correct. The man's wife was indeed with her young lover in the study. The paramour was a guy of about thirty. Bald and looking like he worked out. But fighting tears when he saw the lady's husband standing there with a man wearing a ski mask and holding a gun at his side. It took him about a minute to figure out that the man in the ski mask didn't work for Dr. Kloberg, but was just there to rob him. What a fucking relief.

The woman, in contrast, didn't seem to get upset at all. She was stark naked when they walked in and she remained so as she looked Bridger right in the eye and said,

"Do you mind if I put some clothes on?" Tough lady.

Amidst the shouting and the accusations and the name-calling, Bridger put the young wife and her lover on the couch, telling the lover to shut up and sit still because the man wouldn't stop whining.

Twice, Dr. Kloberg turned around from the wall safe to say something to his wife before Bridger told him to just get on with it.

Then the safe was open. Bridger made Kloberg step back and take a seat on the couch. There, the woman gave him one sharp look and Bridger could tell that the old man would not attempt to hit her. Afraid of her even at this moment. *Geez,* Bridger thought, *all this money and he's not smart enough to stay away from the young stuff.*

Bridger removed a half-million dollars' worth of black diamonds from the safe. They were smaller than Chicklets. He put them in his pocket along with the earrings. He turned to the people on the couch.

"I'm going to have to tie you up. If any of you need to go to the bathroom, tell me now. If you have some sort of medical problem, tell me now."

The young lover asked if he could be allowed to just leave. Like it was a reasonable request because it wasn't his home. Bridger said no.

"Okay," Bridger said, and began the job of tying them up. He said, "I presume someone will be here in the morning."

"Yes," the lady said. Again looking right into his ski mask, Jesus, a hint of a smile on her face. "The maid. She'll get here at eight o'clock." Cold-blooded, this one.

"Good," Bridger said. "She'll untie you and then you can do what you need to do." He did not tell them that the phone lines had been cut.

Bridger found two cell phones. One in the pocket of the young lover's pants and another in the woman's purse. He put them in his jacket pockets. He went back to the young man's pants and removed a set of car keys.

Bridger said, "Which car is yours?"

"It's the white Porsche."

Bridger sighed. Not the most inconspicuous vehicle. But then it would not seem out of place in this neighborhood. Always blend in when you can. Bridger put the keys in his pocket.

Then he started to leave.

The old man called out to him.

"Hey," he said.

"What?" Bridger asked.

"I'll give you a hundred thousand to kill them. Shoot them both."

The young lover's mouth dropped and his eyes widened like saucers. "Jesus, Richard —"

The woman seemed unruffled. What she did was turn and look at her husband, her mouth a thin smile of contempt. Her husband could not meet her eye.

Bridger said, "That's not my thing."

And saw the woman's smile broaden. The woman turned to Bridger and said, "A man of principle, huh?"

"Right," Bridger said, wondering if he was addressing the reincarnation of Joan Crawford. If he stayed any longer, she'd probably persuade him to shoot himself.

Dr. Kloberg said to him, "You see what I have to deal with?"

Bridger shrugged and said, "People get upset, they say things they don't mean."

He walked out of the room and left them to it.

He dropped the Porsche off in the parking lot of a shopping mall in Mount Vernon. He walked to the other side of the parking lot that was by the movie theater and got into a used Buick Park Avenue. His work car. It had New York plates. He put the attaché case in the trunk, but kept the diamonds in his pockets.

He drove to a closed bar and grill a mile away, parked behind it, and looked to see if there was anyone around. There wasn't. He took off the jacket and tie and shirt. For a few moments, he wore only a T-shirt, pants and shoes. He threw the jacket and tie and shirt into a dumpster. From the trunk of the Buick, he removed a sweatshirt and a pair of jeans. He switched from the suit slacks to the jeans and put on the sweat-shirt. He threw the suit slacks into the dumpster along with the shoes. He took a pair of rain boots out of the trunk and put them on his feet. When this was done, he got back in the car.

As planned, by the time he was driving the Buick, he was in morning traffic. One of a million people driving to work. By eight A.M., he was on the New Jersey Turnpike. Then took I-95 to Baltimore. Which was where he lived.

Bridger owned a small garage near the Dundalk Marine Terminals. The garage was not registered in his name. He unlocked the garage door and drove the Buick in. He stored the attaché case and its tools behind a secret wall. When that was done, he got in a blue '74 two-door Chevy Nova. Started it and drove it out of the garage. He stopped outside and went back to lock the door, then got back in the Nova and drove away. He looked forward to getting home and getting some sleep.

The diamonds were in the pocket of his jeans.

Two

Blanco knew it wasn't good when he got the call from D'Andrea the night before. D'Andrea had only said, "We need to talk." No harsh language, no raised voice, but the tone was such that Blanco knew he was in trouble.

Henry D'Andrea recently became an acting captain in the Tessa crime family, operating out of New York. The Tessas had branches operating out of Philadelphia and Miami. Philly was under Nick Blanco's watch. Henry knew it and Nick Blanco knew that he knew.

Henry D'Andrea drove his Lexus to the long-term parking garage of the Newark International Airport. He got into an Oldsmobile Bravada that had been left in the garage for him and drove back out. He peeled off the New Jersey Turnpike at the I-278 exit, then headed southwest down to Route 1 toward Trenton. When he stopped the car, it was at a high school in suburb land, somewhere between the Princeton Battlefields and the New Jersey state capitol.

He took a seat in the stands on the side of a baseball practice field. High school boys were on the field, warming up for morning practice as best they could in the March chill.

Ten to fifteen minutes later, Nick Blanco took a seat next to him.

Blanco was a handsome man. He dressed well and used firm hold gel on his hair. Henry D'Andrea had a Teamster's face, thick and melon-like, bald on top with hair on the sides. Like a monk.

They acknowledged each other, using first names. D'Andrea kept his eyes on the field, like the players had interested him.

After some moments of this, Nick Blanco said, "What's on your mind, Henry?" A little bold on Blanco's part, but he wasn't going to be intimidated into confessing things he didn't know about.

D'Andrea said, "We've got a very serious fucking problem."

"What is it?"

"What is it," D'Andrea said. Laying that out now. "It's your man. Vince."

"Vince Salvetti?"

"Yeah."

"What about him?"

"He's a fed."

For a moment, Nick Blanco didn't say anything. Then he laughed.

"Henry, come on. Whaddaya . . . Vince?"

Nick Blanco pictured Vince Salvetti. Big, dumb, Italian rockhead. Stood around in his mechanic's coveralls with his hands in his pockets. Looking stupid . . . singing to himself, sometimes. *Ain't that a kick in the head.* Stuff like that. Blanco said, "You're shitting me."

"No, Nick, I am not shitting you."

"Henry, you've met Vince, right?"

"Yeah."

"Then you know the guy's a fucking two-by-four. He's got a watch on his wrist, you ask him the time, he looks up at the sky, for Christ's sake; like he's got to think about it. I mean the guy's just not fucking bright."

"His name's not Vince," D'Andrea said. "He's not Vince Salvetti. His name is John Morano. He's not from Jersey. He's from California, and he graduated from the FBI Academy in Quantico five years ago. He's a fed, Nick. And you've had him right under your fucking nose for two fucking years."

It was actually less than that, Nick Blanco thought. But only a little less. *Christ.* It couldn't be possible. He felt his body

25

temperature rising and a twinge in his stomach. If it was true, the Tessas would hold him responsible for it. If it was true, it could be bad. Very bad. Nick Blanco thought at that moment, *If they wanted to kill me, they would not have sent Henry. They'd've just done it.*

Blanco said, "How do you know this?" Putting some back into it now.

D'Andrea seemed to regard him for a moment before shaking his head. As if to say, don't think you're going to bluff your way out of this one, *spaching.* "We *know,* Nick," he said.

"But —"

"But nothing. Listen to me. Two weeks ago, your boys did that thing in Boston?"

"Yeah?"

"Well, you were gone for a while." D'Andrea paused to let that sink in a bit, adding that grievance to some list he'd already compiled. He said, "While you were gone, they found the security guard and were trying to get him tied up. The guy was getting all frantic and Jimmy was saying they were gonna put a couple in his head, but Vince stepped in and said, 'Let me talk to him.' Went over to the security guard and said something to him. Got him calmed down."

"What did he say?"

"Well, Jimmy didn't hear that. But that's not the point."

"What is the point?"

"I said Jimmy didn't hear what he said. But Jimmy saw how Vince talked to the security guard and as he said, it wasn't Vince. He meant, it was Vince in person, you see, but Vince was different when he calmed down that security guard. See, Vince stepped out of character. And Jimmy's not fucking stupid. Jimmy notices things like that."

"That's it?" Nick Blanco said. Like it wasn't much.

"So nothing. Maybe Jimmy's paranoid. Maybe he's just nervous on the job and he's jumping at shadows. But he told us and we had to look into it."

Nick Blanco said, "He never said nothing to me."

"Yeah?" D'Andrea said. "And what would you have done?" Giving him the hard-on now.

Nick Blanco didn't answer.

"So," D'Andrea said, "we did some checking. Made some calls and what-not."

"Maybe it's a —"

"And found out that he's a fed. Special Agent John Morano of the FBI."

The boys on the field were an inning into their scrimmage now. A rangy fourteen-year-old kid was on the pitcher's mound, staring at the batter with an intensity of a major-league starter. It was something, but not everything. The coach kept yelling, "Throw strikes."

Henry D'Andrea said, "It's a bad situation, Nick."

"I'll fix it."

"How are you going to fix it?"

"He'll have an accident."

At the plate, the batter got a hold of one and blooped it out between second base and left field. The pitching coach could be heard groaning.

D'Andrea said, "Well, that's a start. But does it take care of it, Nick? Does it take care of everything?"

"I'll clean it up, Henry. All of it." Nick Blanco was not going to let the man frighten him. If he wanted to plug him, he could do it right now, but Nick wasn't going to lay prostrate before him. Nick said, "Anything else?"

D'Andrea kept his eyes on the field. "No," he said. "Give me an update in a couple of days."

Nick Blanco left the man on the stands.

THREE

Bridger lived in a row house off York Road in the Rodgers Forge section of North Baltimore. The house had a red brick front with ivy and shrubs covering part of it and it was on a narrow, one-way street with cars parked on both sides. You could drive one car up the street at a time; it was that narrow. There was a garage behind the house that could be accessed only through the alley.

The neighborhood had changed over the years. A generation ago it had housed line workers for G.M. and union employees from the Giant Food store. Now it housed young doctors and lawyers and bond traders, buying their first homes before moving on. The Chevys and Fords had been replaced by Saabs and Lexus SUVs.

It was a nice place to live.

A kid rode a skateboard down the sidewalk, another kid on a bicycle following him, yelling something.

It was about three in the afternoon when Bridger got out of bed, showered and dressed. There was no woman next to him in the bed, no one downstairs waiting for him. He lived alone.

He descended the stairs and went out the back door and backed the Nova out of the garage. He stopped the car where the alley intersected with the street, looked both ways before turning right. Drove past St. Pius church and started north on York Road.

He soon passed the Baltimore Beltway and continued north. The city and its suburban commercial sites drifted behind him and before long he was in Maryland horse country. Estates, rolling hills, lush green grounds that are still the beauty of that state, a distinct culture that is not quite south and not quite north.

Now Bridger was driving on a narrow, blacktopped lane parallel to a wooden white fence. The fence coming into sharper focus as Bridger slowed the car and took in the sight of a pretty girl riding a chestnut bay. The girl wore jeans and riding boots and a dark blue sweater. Monfort's daughter, Bridger thought. Probably a college student by now.

Bridger came to the long drive that led to

Monfort's house and turned in and drove up to where the driveway ended in a semi-circle in front. A brown Range Rover was parked at the apex.

Bridger got out of the Nova as Alan Monfort came out of the house.

Monfort said, "You should think about getting another car."

"I like this one," Bridger said.

Alan Monfort shook his head. "I don't know why you do that. You could be driving a new Mercedes if you want."

Bridger didn't respond.

"I know," Monfort said. "A class thing, right? Come on in."

Later, they were standing next to a counter in the kitchen. High-dollar pots and pans hung from the ceiling. An Orioles game on the radio. Spread out on the counter were the black diamonds Bridger had brought.

Alan Monfort had his diamond gauge out and a jeweler's glass in his eye.

Bridger held a mug of hot coffee in his hand, its aroma drifting up and out.

Alan put down the jeweler's glass. He said, "I can give you a hundred and ten for these."

Bridger sipped his coffee.

Alan said, "I could get more if you wanted

31

to wait a couple of months. Do you want to do that?"

"No," Bridger said. "Do you have it now?" Meaning, cash.

"I have fifty. I can get you the rest tomorrow." Alan said, "Do you want to bring this back tomorrow?"

"No. I'll leave it with you. What time tomorrow?"

"Eleven in the morning should be all right. Come by then."

"Okay," Bridger said.

In the driveway, Bridger stopped the car as Monfort's daughter walked her horse in front of him. She was holding the reins and she looked at him through the windshield and almost smiled. Then she was out of the way and Bridger drove on.

He took the Jones Falls Expressway back into the city and pulled up to a rundown automotive garage near Hampden forty minutes later. It was a different garage from the one he kept near the waterfront. There was a faded red and white sign that said *A&T Automotive Repair.* There were three cars parked on the side, all foreign. There were two bays, both doors open. In one of them a Vietnamese man was standing next to the exposed engine of a '98 BMW 740iL.

A black guy wearing a jacket and tie stood on the other side of the car, leaning against it, hoping the mechanic wouldn't tell him something bad. But the mechanic, whose name was Sonny Ma, was shaking his head as he looked at the handheld computer and repeated what it told him.

"Transmission," Sonny said.

The black guy said, "You sure?"

"Yeah."

"What's that going to cost?"

"A lot. I don't do transmissions."

The black guy said, "Aww . . ." He was trying not to swear.

Sonny acknowledged Bridger who was now standing next to the customer. Bridger said, "You need to go to AAMCO or a place like that. Or the dealer. You're probably better off with a new one than you would be a rebuild."

"Man . . ."

Sonny said, "These bitches cost you money." He was shaking his head again.

Bridger gestured to the Toyota in the other bay. "That one waiting?"

"Yeah," Sonny said. "Water pump."

"You got the part here?"

"Yeah. It's on the workbench."

Bridger changed into coveralls in the small office at the back of the garage and went to

33

work on the Toyota. Time passed and soon it was five-thirty and the owner of the Toyota returned to pick up her car. Bridger had finished it by then. He took the lady's check in the office and told her the things customers like to hear from their mechanics. He told her she shouldn't hear that screeching, chattering sound anymore. She thanked him a second time and drove off the lot.

Bridger walked out of the garage. Sonny was leaning against a car, taking a break and smoking a cigarette and looking off to the west.

The garage was registered in Sonny's name, but the seed money for the business had been supplied by Bridger. Sonny had evacuated Vietnam on a boat when he was a child. His sister and mother had been with him, his father killed by the Communists. Sonny had had a tough life and he didn't ask Bridger questions he didn't want the answers to. Though more than once he'd asked Bridger when he was going to get married and have kids. Sonny said that a man comes home from work tired but then plays with his kids and he not feel so tired anymore. He turned to Bridger now, aware of his presence, and gestured to his package of cigarettes. Bridger said, no thanks.

An older model Mercedes coupe pulled into the lot. The engine pitched higher as its gear was moved into park and then shut off. A pair of slim legs swung out of the driver's side and then an attractive Chinese woman in her thirties was standing next to the car.

Bridger said, "Hello, Maggie."

"Bridger," Maggie Chan said. She remained by the car for a moment, taking Bridger and his coveralls in.

"You need an oil change?" Bridger said.

Maggie Chan shook her head. She acknowledged Sonny with a nod and said his name. Sonny said her name back and looked back off to the west.

Maggie said, "I thought we might have a drink. Are you busy tonight?"

"No. I'm dirty though."

"Get cleaned up."

"Then what?"

"The Mount Royal? In an hour?"

"Okay, Maggie."

She moved back toward the Mercedes. "I see you then," she said over her shoulder.

FOUR

Termane picked Foo-Foo up at the 30th Street Station. They exchanged greetings and Termane drove the Honda Accord away from the lot. They took the Schuykill Expressway down to the South Street Bridge and crossed the river into South Philly.

It was Foo-Foo that had called Termane Goode Jr. and said that a man was going to pay them ten thousand dollars to kill someone. A white man named Vincent, name ending in a vowel. Killing a wop for another wop. It was a job. Foo-Foo told Termane he'd give him half the money but Termane was to bring the vehicle and the guns and not fuck it up. Termane was to be ready to go in one hour tops, and if he couldn't do that he needed to tell Foo-Foo right now. Termane told Foo-Foo to stop trying to be a hard-talking nigger and just tell him where they needed to meet and what sort of guns did he want.

Twenty-twos, Foo-Foo said. The kind that don't jam. And Termane said, you mean revolvers? And Foo-Foo said, yeah, that's what he had just said.

Termane Goode Jr. shook his head at the phone. Termane could go into Center City at seven A.M. empty-handed and come out at seven-thirty with whatever guns you needed and an Egg McMuffin to go. Foo-Foo couldn't and the man would never say so.

The name on Foo-Foo's birth certificate was Kenneth Samson. The name on Termane's was the same one he used. Two men, age twenty-seven and twenty-four, respectively, whose long-term thinking did not extend beyond two weeks.

In the car Termane said, "They pay you up front?"

Foo-Foo said, "No, man. The man gave me two thousand, said we get the rest on delivery. He good for it."

"Yeah? Why don't he give you half?"

"Man, I was lucky to get the two. These motherfuckers, they think you give a nigger five thousand dollars you ain't ever gonna see him again. Think he be out blowing it on ripple and pussy."

"You said they was Italians, right?"

"Yeah, man. They're fucking animals."

37

"Why they having us do it?"

"Hell, I don't know. Who cares?" Foo-Foo gestured to a black canvas bag on the floorboard in front of his seat. "In here?"

"Yeah."

Foo-Foo opened up the bag and found two black twenty-two revolvers along with two full boxes holding fifty cartridges each.

Foo-Foo said, "Damn, boy. You think we're going to Beirut or something?"

"You complaining 'cause I got too much? You want, I can take it back right now."

Foo-Foo ignored him. They were driving slowly through the South Philly neighborhood now. Small junk lots selling used tires gave way to funeral homes and dark brick houses with metal awnings. Foo-Foo gave a series of directions and soon they were parked in front of a three-story walk-up apartment building. They stayed in the car and they waited for an hour while Termane smoked cigarettes and dropped ash out the window. Foo-Foo kept his eye on the building.

In the second hour, a thick-set man came out of the front door and walked down the steps.

Foo-Foo leaned forward in his seat.

Then said, "That's him. Put that in your pocket." Meaning the gun.

They watched the man walk away from the apartment building and go down the street.

Termane said, "Should we go now?"

"No," Foo-Foo said. "He might see us and start running. I don't want to run after him." *He might be armed too,* Foo-Foo thought, but kept that to himself.

Termane said, "What then?"

"Just wait a minute. I'll tell you what to do." Letting the man know this was his job and he was no more than second-in-command. "Start the car, follow him . . . don't get past him."

Foo-Foo was looking at the man now, his eyes focused like a wildcat's, almost willing the man to walk where Foo-Foo wanted him to walk. Where he believed the man was going to walk.

And the man did, too, walking into the bodega at the end of the block. A corner bodega that probably had one way in and one way out.

"Okay," Foo-Foo said, his heart beating now. "Let's go."

A corner bodega with chips and drinks and six-packs of beer and nasty-tasting sandwiches wrapped in plastic. There was a Vietnamese man behind the counter.

John Morano, aka Vince Salvetti, was

standing in the second aisle fingering through the Philadelphia *Daily Bulletin*. Foo-Foo came in the store and gestured for Termane to stay by the door. Foo-Foo rounded the corner into the second aisle. It was a small store and within two steps he was standing within five feet of Morano. Foo-Foo pulled the pistol out of his jacket pocket.

Morano saw the flash of black steel. His eyes widened and as he was starting to say "hey," Foo-Foo shot him in the face. John Morano went down and Foo-Foo leaned over him and put the muzzle of the pistol against his head and pulled the trigger four times.

The Vietnamese man ducked behind the counter when he heard the shots. Termane was distracted by the crack of gunfire and didn't notice the man dropping to the ground. He turned back to face the counter and saw that the Vietnamese cashier was gone. Termane jumped up onto the counter and pulled his pistol out to kill the man, leaned over to see where he was —

— and saw the man lying on his back pointing a gun up at him.

The Vietnamese man was holding a Sig Sauer semi-automatic that he had bought in New Mexico. He pulled the trigger twice and shot Termane Goode Jr. twice in the chest, the Vietnamese man crying out as he did it.

Termane Goode Jr. fell back on the other side of the counter.

Foo-Foo came out of the aisle to see Termane lying on the ground with his chest opened up and red and meaty. Termane moaning and sounding like he was having trouble breathing.

"Jesus," Foo-Foo said. "Jesus."

Thought, *what happened?*

It was all too fast. Termane on the ground with life coming out of him, his gun by his side. It was all too fast. Gun blasts from somewhere and Termane was not long for anything. The man not able to even form words.

Foo-Foo ran out of the store.

Between twenty and thirty minutes later, there were police and other emergency personnel stuffed into the bodega. A small crowd forming outside. Detectives in plain-clothes were trying to take a statement from the Vietnamese owner of the store who was crying and saying he'd never shot anybody before. The paramedics went to work on the man that was still alive, the black man that had been shot by the proprietor, but he

41

was dead before they could even get him on a stretcher.

They found identification on the white man in the aisle and a .38 snubnose in a holster on his ankle. The lead detective saw that holster and thought, *cop.* And hoped he was wrong. Though the victim was no one he recognized.

The lead detective found out later that evening that he was right, though, when his captain called him at home and said the victim was a special agent of the FBI. The captain told the lead detective to double-check his reports because the both of them were to meet with men from the Philadelphia branch of the FBI at eight o'clock the next morning.

The captain said, "And you know how those guys are. Like as not, they'll try to find some way to blame this on us."

FIVE

The Mount Royal Tavern was narrow and dark and had high ceilings. You walked up a steep set of stairs to get in. Inside, an art student was sitting at the bar with a chessboard in front of him, his bookbag on the floor. The bartender playing him. The smell of years of cigarette smoke and beer. A song came from the jukebox; Willie singing you've no more money, honey, I've no more time.

Bridger sat with the good-looking Chinese lady in a booth near the back of the tavern. An eight-ounce bottle of Coca-Cola in front of him, no glass. Maggie Chan sipping a Manhattan, her only one of the night. Neither one of them were heavy drinkers.

Maggie said, "It's a coin collection."

Bridger said, "Where?"

"Philadelphia. The Main Line. You know it?"

Bridger had pulled two jobs there. One of

which Maggie knew about. He said, "I know it."

Maggie Chan knew things. She had been a dancer at a club in South Baltimore when she was eighteen. A prostitute for the better part of her twenties. Got out of that life when she hooked up with Jack McGurn, an enforcer in the Dundalk rackets. Jack McGurn made Maggie his wife. She took his name and shared his home near Fell's Point and their two years together were not unpleasant. In part, this was because Maggie went in with both eyes open. She knew Jack was not much of a long-term prospect. But she also knew, at least at that stage in her life, they were not long-term prospect sort of people. Besides, Jack was fun and he genuinely cared about her and liked her.

Even before they got married — when they started living together — Maggie took to hiding money from him. Hers and his. She felt no guilt about this. She did not consider it stealing, but rather a measure of self-protection. Everyone knew Jack liked to gamble. On anything. Horses, cards, football games, how much snow there would be on the ground at seven A.M. And so forth. Maggie knew of several twenty-thousand-dollar beatings her husband had taken at the blackjack table. Knew how quickly it could happen. Start at around nine, nine-thirty and at midnight he would be twenty grand poorer. The next morning, asking, did I really do that? Then doing it again ten days later. Maggie saw the writing on the wall before Jack did, though she kept her mouth shut. A little mercenary on her part, but she knew it wouldn't have done any good to warn him. Jack never listened to anybody.

Sure enough, Jack began racking debts up with the Outfit. Threats were made. Then more threats, the nature of them escalating. Until eventually Jack made the mistake that many organization men make: overestimating his value. Specifically, he began to let it be known that he wasn't getting what he was worth and, worse, he reminded them that he knew where bodies were buried. Literally.

He lasted about a week after that. His body was found floating in the Patapsco River.

At the funeral, Maggie shook hands with men she was moderately sure had had Jack killed. She held no grudges. One of them said, "It's just a fucking shame. Everybody loved Jackie." Tears rolling down his cheeks when he said it. Maggie believed the man's grief was genuine. It was the life they were in, and there was no point in scoffing at ironies.

After that, Maggie McGurn went back to being Maggie Chan. Opened a small business that had a sign that said, "Photos — Passport/Identification." An older and wiser woman then, no longer a dancer, no longer a whore.

Maggie knew Bridger before her husband died. They were two people who knew they wanted to sleep with each other within five minutes of their first meeting. But they were both, in their way, pragmatists. Maggie did not wish to be unfaithful to Jack. And Bridger had never been one to start a fight with a mobster.

Bridger waited one month after the funeral before he called Maggie. The first thing she said was, "I was wondering when I was going to hear from you." Bridger had smiled and they met the next night at a hotel in Glen Burnie.

Odd, that. Sneaking around, like married people. Worried about being spotted by one of Jack's friends. Maybe even by the same ones who had been involved in having him whacked. But you never knew about those guys and their bizarre sense of loyalty and family.

A few years had passed since then and

they were not as cautious as they used to be. Connected to each other, though not really connected. Perhaps both of them incapable of such things.

Now Bridger said, "A coin collection."

"Yes," Maggie said. "A four-million-dollar coin collection. I have someone in Chicago — I won't tell you who — he'll give us twenty percent. That's eight hundred thousand dollars, split between you and I."

"An even split?"

"Those are my terms."

"And I take all the risk, right?"

Maggie Chan said, "You're a big fellah."

Bridger took a drink of his Coke.

"Well," he said, "that sounds great on paper. But how do I know it's there?"

"I have good information."

"Well ain't that a comfort. From who?"

Maggie shook her head.

Bridger said, "You don't make things easy."

"Danny, you're better off not knowing. You get caught and . . ." She made a gesture.

"And I'll talk?"

"Not about me," Maggie said. Smiled. "Maybe not about me. But the flesh is weak, huh."

Bridger said, "You don't trust anyone, do you?"

"No. But I like you. I like you very much."

"All right, that's enough. Is there something else?"

"Man," Maggie said, her eyebrows raising. "Talk about not trusting. Yes. As a matter of fact, there is something else."

"What?"

"It must be done tomorrow night."

Bridger studied her for a moment, searching for a tell. A weakness. He didn't find one in that tough, lovely face. "Why?" he said.

"I am informed that the collection will be moved the day after . . . that's how they know where it is."

Bridger tried to smile it away. "I . . . don't like that. That gives me no time to do groundwork."

"It's an easy job. You wait until dark and everybody's asleep and you walk in and take it and walk out. Besides, Philly's a two-hour drive from here. You could be there at eight in the morning. That's enough time to do your scouting."

"No, it's not."

Maggie Chan smiled. She had smiled at him that way before. He was old enough to know better, but he didn't. She said, "Then say no."

"Maybe I will."

Still smiling, Maggie said, "Maybe . . ."

Ten minutes later they were making love in the storage room. Bridger's pants around his ankles, Maggie's skirt hiked up, her panties somewhere on the cement floor, her body wrapped around him as she gripped the cases of stacked beer to steady herself. Maggie getting there and then crying out when she did, Bridger saying "ssshh" again and again so no one would hear them on the other side of the door.

Six

Joe Hannon would make jokes and the patrons would laugh. Lawyers, most of them, who knew him from court. Some of them had supported his reelection, some had not. Those who had not kept quiet. There were some who donated to all the judges' campaigns, covering all their bets. Hard, clipped laughter of men of ambition and fear. It didn't matter to Judge Hannon. His was not an insightful nature. It was all a game, anyway. Life and politics. It was not something you should take too seriously. Laugh at the bad jokes, at the jibes that were more flattery than anything else, go along with the code words and gestures of men and women wanting to show that they were all part of the Success Club. What did it matter, anyway? They were in his place, his restaurant, *his* club. They were laughing and drinking and eating good food, looking up at him as he went around the tables, placing hands on shoulders and asking if everything was all right. It was a good life.

The name of the restaurant was *Frères-Laval.* It had a dark atmosphere, smoking allowed in the bar area. Wine-colored walls and chairs with red velvet covers. Small violet-colored lamps hanging over the dining tables.

The name referred to the Laval brothers, Henri and Robert. Who had left Grenoble in the fifties to look for America and later found themselves in Philadelphia. Robert fell in love with the place; married a girl from the Main Line who fell in love with his hair and his voice and the way he smoked a cigarette. Existential, *non?* For Henri, not so much. He went back to France after fifteen years and would tell the W. C. Fields joke to puzzled Frenchmen the rest of his days. First prize — one week in Philadelphia. Second prize — two weeks in Philadelphia.

In the sixties, the brothers opened the restaurant that would become known as the best French bistro on the Main Line. The name remained after Henri sold Robert his share; "Robert's" could not be spelled in such a way to demonstrate French cuisine. It could only be pronounced, not written. Robert's lovely American wife died of cancer in the nineties and he followed her to the grave a year and a half later.

Now, pan across from the loud Irish-American politician holding court at the table . . . to the marble-topped bar where his wife Claire Laval serves Calvados to a couple quietly celebrating their twenty-second wedding anniversary. Claire Laval has kept her maiden name. Perhaps out of respect for her father, perhaps thinking it is bad karma for the owner of a French restaurant to have an Irish last name. She is the only child of Robert Laval and the actual owner of the restaurant, though she allows her husband to say things like, "our place."

In her thirties now, dark hair falling to her shoulders. She has a Frenchwoman's trim, petite figure, obtained by a lifestyle of European diet and moderate eating habits inherited from her father. She has never been a member of a gym. A natural beauty, without makeup or cosmetic surgery. She thinks breast implants are barbaric and done to compete with other women. She is a bit of a contemporary Edith Wharton, not quite French and not quite American, and she hasn't quite figured out where she belongs.

The couple celebrating their anniversary were regular customers. She liked them both, though was somewhat partial to the man. He was a banker. He had a gentle disposition and seemed to know when his wife was saying too much. Tonight, he said, "I'd like to think that you're working the bar tonight for us."

Claire smiled. "I am."

"Don't flatter an old man," he said. "Angie have the night off?"

"No. She has the flu." Claire said, "I don't mind it."

The man's wife said, "Is she okay?"

"She will be. It's just a stomach flu."

"It's going around," the woman said. "It happens when the weather changes." She turned to her husband. "Jennifer's coming down with something too." She said to Claire, "Our daughter."

Claire nodded. She knew that already. Jennifer, now a student at Penn State, one of their three children.

Claire Laval looked across the restaurant at her husband. Joe Hannon was wearing a starched white shirt, open at the collar, and dark slacks. She looked at him and felt a bit of a void. Jealous, suddenly, of this woman in front of her. A woman who was not pretty or interesting, but a woman who had children and something of substance with this man.

Claire mentally shook her head. *What's wrong with you?* she thought. It was not her way to get wistful and self-pitying. An old couple comes into the restaurant to celebrate their anniversary and you feel envy and sadness?

But I don't want to be divorced again.

That was what it was. She wanted to think that it was all complicated. That she and Joe had deep issues that were complicated and the result of different goals and ambitions and worldviews. All of which may have been true. But . . . so what? She knew that when she married him. She knew they were two different people, and even as a young girl in college she had not believed in the concept of "soul mates."

Her father had said that the French, the most romantic people in the world, did not marry for love. They did not delude themselves that way. They married to start families. They went in *understanding,* he said. Understanding the way things were. Perhaps this led to mistresses and guiltless adultery, but the divorce rate and the abortion rate were lower in France than America. Present at Francois Mitterand's funeral were his wife and his longtime mistress. Something you will never see in America, he said.

But, Claire thought, Robert was somewhat full of shit on that score. Certainly he had worshipped her mother. And though Claire had loved her mother, the fierce adoration he had had for his wife had always been something of a mystery to Claire. At times she believed that her mother had married her father because, at the time, he had been a novelty. A young, dashing Frenchman with long hair and cigarettes. To Claire, he had been something more than that.

She found herself contemplating these things on this the wedding anniversary of patrons of her bistro.

I don't want to be divorced again.

She met her first husband in college. Villanova University. His name had been Cliff. A journalism major who wrote long, impassioned essays calling for divestiture from South Africa and spent a night in a campus shanty to show solidarity. She moved in with him in their senior year. Married him during his first year of law school. They lived on her earnings — she was working for a small advertising agency then — while he studied contracts and torts. It was that or move in with her parents and have an *All in the Family* lifestyle. Eventually, Cliff seemed to become the Meathead himself. Earnest and studious, genuinely concerned with graduating in the top five percent of his class.

It didn't happen. The bottom line was, he wasn't that smart. And this epiphany was not something he was going to accept gracefully. He began to take it out on her. Insults, long punitive silences, suggestions that she wasn't smart enough to understand the subjects he was learning, condescension and more condescension. Then one night, she caught him taking money out of her purse. He did not bother to apologize, but started cross-examining her to demonstrate that it was *their* money, meaning, his money. Trotting out one and a half years of legal training as if he were Clarence Darrow, unaware of how foolish he sounded. After his third question, she said, "Oh, go fuck yourself." More tired than angry when she said it. But it was the first time she'd ever used language like that to argue with him, and she did not like hearing herself talk that way. She left that night, taking her purse with her.

Moved back in temporarily with her parents. Her father said, "I am not surprised." Not meaning to be cruel, but showing that he'd always thought Cliff to be a lowbrow poser.

Claire Laval, divorced at twenty-seven. Feeling ashamed and parochial for feeling the shame.

Around that time, Robert asked her to help manage the restaurant. She did and eventually started doing it full time. It was hard work, but Robert was getting older and he needed her there. She found that she liked it.

Years went by. She did not have much time for a social life. She gave little thought to remarrying. She maintained a cool, aloof air to keep the staff and clientele from coming onto her. Polite, thin smiles at bawdy jokes and suggestions, letting them know she wasn't interested.

When she met Joe Hannon, the first thing he said was, "You're a cool one, aren't you?" She smiled back at him and let him do his schtick. Let him take his time. She was aware that he was a charmer and cultivated a reputation as something of a rogue. But he managed to make her laugh. And she knew that he knew he was one of the few people who could do that.

Her father said, "Another fucking lawyer."

But he was wrong about Joe. Cliff was working at some state agency in Harrisburg now. Joe Hannon was a judge. Apart from having law degrees, they could not have been more different. Cliff was serious and insecure, while John was confidence in human form. Fun and funny, a natural politician. One desired by a lot of women. Claire Laval had enough feminine vanity to enjoy being selected over any of them, some of them prettier than her.

One night she said, "So what is it, Joe?"

"What is what?"

"What do you want from me? A conquest? The knowledge that you and you alone managed to crack the girl at Frères-Laval? Is that what this is about?"

"You misunderstand me, Miss Laval. I want to marry you."

"Shut up."

"I do. I have from the moment I first saw you."

"You're drunk."

"Intoxicated, not drunk."

Claire laughed. "God help me. You actually *say* these things."

"I love you, Claire. Don't give me an answer now. I'll keep asking and in time you'll know I mean it."

After her father died, she agreed to it. She would later tell herself that what cinched it was the way Joe conducted himself at the funeral. Attentive, compassionate, appropriately somber. Helpful. Claire thought, *Mother would have loved him.*

Six years later, wasn't he still the same

man? What was wrong with him now? Had he really changed, or had she? Was she a selfish, overgrown adolescent wishing for too much, asking for too much? He had never hit her, never said anything truly ugly to her. Why, then, had they drifted? What was it that she had done wrong? Why did she have this vague feeling that it was all a masquerade?

Joe was coming over to the bar. She did not feel disloyal with her thoughts; that sort of feeling had passed some time ago.

Claire said, "Hey."

"Hey," Joe said. "Give me another Chardonnay."

Claire noticed that he would not make eye contact with her. *He's still your husband,* she thought. She said, "Is something the matter?"

"No," Joe said. Then looked at her. "Well . . . I just heard about a man getting shot in South Philly. He's dead."

"Was it someone we knew?"

"No. I mean, I met him once. Through some people. But, no, I didn't know him."

She wanted to ask him again: is something the matter? But she was pouring the wine for him, delaying it, thinking about it, and again she thought, *He's your husband.* She set the wineglass on the bar.

59

"Joe —"

"What, Claire?"

The way he said it, like she was being a nuisance. Get to the point. A shittiness in his tone. A practiced lawyer, an authoritative judge; he was a man that used his voice effectively. It pissed her off when he did it outside the courtroom.

"Nothing." She said, "I love you."

"I love you, too," he said. Still not making eye contact. He walked back into the main dining room.

SEVEN

Nick Blanco believed that the next twenty-four hours would be the longest of his life. He wanted to advance the clock one day forward and have it all behind him. But at the same time, he needed to have it slowed down so he could put everything in place and make sure it got done right. His life depended on getting it right, and he would only have one shot. If everything went as planned, he would be all right. He would retain control of the Philadelphia branch of the Tessa operations. If it didn't go right, they would have him killed. D'Andrea had made that plain. And D'Andrea didn't know the half of it. Maybe if he did, he would have had Nick Blanco killed already.

What D'Andrea didn't know:

Vince Salvetti, aka John Morano, had made deliveries of cash to a local district judge, funneling it into the man's restaurant, turning heroin profits into food-servicing profits. Laundering it. Christ.

When Nick thought of it now, he almost had to admire the fucking rat. Judge Hannon had taken a one-hundred-thousand dollar bribe on a drug trafficking case two years ago. So the man was an easy mark. But as Nick thought back on it, it seemed to be less clear that it was his idea to approach Hannon on the laundering than it was Vince's. Vince had merely said, "Joe's a good guy," and Nick had taken it from there. They had probably washed close to three hundred thousand dollars through the man's restaurant. Naturally, Nick had allowed people to think that it had been his — Nick's — idea. He took the credit, as the rat-fed knew he would.

Christ. The fed had done a number on him.

Now Nick was wondering, *But was it me the feds were after? Or was it the judge?*

A guinea operator out of South Philly, sure, that would get attention. But to bring down a judge? That would be front-page material. A convicted judge would get the agent a centerfold in whatever it was they read.

It was the judge Vince had been after. The fucking judge was going to get them all pinched.

What was it the poet had said? Something about keeping your head about you when all the fucking rats are swimming away from the sinking ship? All right, then. Looking at this thing positively, Nick convinced himself that he had gotten lucky. If D'Andrea hadn't got wind of the fed, he would have eventually pinched Hannon and the rest of them would have gone down with him. Conspiracy charges to begin with. Hannon had not been aware of any murders, but the feds were ambitious and the end result would still be a federal penitentiary in Texas or some other uncivilized desert.

Earlier he had told D'Andrea he'd clean it up. And he would. More than D'Andrea would ever know.

He felt a little better when Foo-Foo called him and told him it was done. At least the fed was rotting in rat-hell. But Foo-Foo's voice was shaking and the cool pimp-daddy attitude was noticeably absent.

Nick Blanco was standing in a phone booth at a Fina station, his Lexus nearby. He said, "What happened?"

Foo-Foo said, "Uh, yeah, well, Termane got shot."

"Jesus Christ. Vince shoot him?"

"No, man. The clerk shot him."

"The clerk — what the fuck are you talking about?" The relieved feeling gone now.

"We were in a bodega and this clerk —"

"What'd you fucking do it there for?"

"We just — the clerk, man, he had a gun apparently and, uh, I think Termane is dead."

"Did you kill him?"

"Who?"

"The clerk, goddammit. Did you kill him?"

"Uh, no. There wasn't time."

"Did Termane make it out of there?"

"Uh . . . no."

Nick Blanco sighed. Fucking moolies. A live witness, a dead accomplice left in the store, probably with his driver's license in his pocket. He imagined D'Andrea lecturing him about it in the near future. *You gave the job to a coupla carjacking niggers? What, are you stupid?* He'd say it before he killed him, getting a point across. *What we have here is a failure of leadership.*

Nick said, "Where are you now?"

"I'm at a pay phone on Carpenter Street."

"Are you okay?"

"Yeah, I'm good."

"Well, let's get you paid up."

"Yeah," Foo-Foo said. "Let's." Being the tough pimp again.

Nick Blanco smiled. The man on the other

64

end was tired and he was scared. He wanted to get paid and get back to Brooklyn where things were familiar to him. Nick decided he would test him.

"I can get it for you first thing tomorrow."

"No, man, fuck that. I need it tonight. Tonight, you hear?"

"Tonight? Fuck me, I can't get it set up tonight."

"We made a deal, brother. I want it tonight."

"All right, all right. How about we meet at the Marine Terminal?"

"When?"

"Midnight. I mean, you can wait that long."

"No longer, man."

"I'll see you then."

An L1011 roared overhead, a red-eye flight going to Boston. The sound of the engines faded out and they could hear the traffic going over the Walt Whitman Bridge. Cold and wet out, the smell of the Delaware River coming through the crack in the window of the car.

An older model Grand Prix with a black vinyl top, its long nose coming to a point.

There were two men inside. Kenny Doolin, the pale-skinned Irishman who was called Kenny D and didn't mind it. He was twenty-six years old and he had seen the Eminem movie three times.

Next to him was a man in his thirties with a bigger build. He wore a leather jacket that hung down past his waist and cost him six hundred dollars. His name was Claude Maddox. He was doing a crossword puzzle, squinting at times to see the clues.

Claude Maddox was aware that Kenny was getting restless, waiting. He was not surprised when Kenny said, "That a crossword puzzle?"

Which anyone could have seen. Maddox said, "Yeah."

"You can do those?"

"Yep."

"Man. I never could learn how to do those. You go to college?"

"No."

Claude Maddox had done an eight-year stretch for involuntary manslaughter. All of it in Graterford State Correctional Institute and he had learned to deal with time. Sitting in a car waiting for midnight to come was a lot better than sitting in a box waiting for years.

Kenny D said, "You watch *Fear Factor* last night?"

"No. I don't have cable."

"You don't have to have cable. It's on network," Kenny D said. "They had this chick on there, big tits, wearing a bikini. Fucking hot chick. She's supposed to drink this milkshake with bugs and shit in it. Grasshoppers. I mean, like real grasshoppers in it. And she starts to drink it, but then she threw up all over her front. It was fucking disgusting."

Maddox did not look up from his puzzle. He said, "Why didn't you turn it off?"

"Fuck, I don't know. Jesus, just trying to have a fucking conversation with you."

Maddox looked at his watch. "It's almost eleven o'clock," he said. "I'm going up on the roof."

He took a SIG-Sauer SG 550 sniper rifle from the backseat floorboard. The rifle was black. It had a folding stock and a thick scope that rested on top.

Maddox said, "Don't turn the radio on or light a cigarette, okay?"

"Don't worry about it."

Nick Blanco was there at quarter till. He parked his car and shut the engine off. He did not leave the lights on.

It was ten minutes after midnight before Foo-Foo showed up. In a Honda Accord and he had someone with him driving it.

Foo-Foo stepped out. His right hand in his pocket.

Nick said, "Keep your hands out of your pocket, Foo-Foo. This is a friendly meeting."

"Yeah, you too, Nick."

Nick Blanco extended his arms out. In his right hand was an 8 × 11 envelope. It looked thick. "Right here, Foo-Foo . . . come on, man. It's cold out here; I want to finish this."

Foo-Foo said, "Bring it over here."

Nick began walking. As he approached, he said, "I'm sorry you lost a man."

Foo-Foo said, "Ah, he knew what he was getting into."

They were closing now, fifteen yards between them.

"Them gooks," Nick said, "they like their guns, man." He raised his right hand above his head.

A bullet pierced Foo-Foo's head. It seemed to bounce with the impact, like it would have been knocked off his body if it hadn't been attached. Foo-Foo went down.

In the Honda, the man behind the wheel saw Foo-Foo hit the ground. He had heard the shot, like a firecracker. He couldn't believe it was happening. He saw the white man with the good clothes take a handgun out of his pocket, the white man facing *him* now, looking at him through the windshield, as he raised the pistol to fire. The man in the car put the gearshift in reverse and stomped the accelerator. The car started moving backward, gaining speed as Nick Blanco began firing shots into the windshield.

Kenny D drove the Grand Prix out from between the shipping crates and cut the Honda off. The Honda smashed into the prow of the Grand Prix, coming to a halt, and now Maddox was firing shots into the windshield too, one after another, as Blanco was walking and firing, and Kenny D jumped out of the Grand Prix, a pistol in his hand, seeing the black guy flinch as a bullet hit him and Kenny D fired three times through the driver's-side window, ending it as all of his shots found their mark.

Kenny D stood next to Nick Blanco.

Kenny said, "Well, that's out of the way."

Nick said, "Don't do any celebrating yet. I'm going to need you for tomorrow."

Soon Maddox was standing with them. Nick Blanco looked at him and nodded and Maddox said, "Well, let's get rid of these bodies."

EIGHT

Bridger drove the Buick to Philadelphia. He got there early, around 8:30 A.M. Driving with the radio on, the local DJs bitching about Terrell Owens and his agent. The radio on, but Bridger not really listening to it, just wanting background noise while he thought about coins.

He had done a job near Denver once that was all coins. A big house up in the mountains. Snow on the ground that would show tracks so he had to move out quickly after he was done. He remembered the dry air had made him nervous for some reason. Perhaps because he wasn't used to it. He had grown up on the East Coast. Six years in the Navy, duty on a ship docking in Subic Bay, the Philippines, places like that. Sailors rushing ashore to get laid, making sure they had condoms before they left the ship. A wet, damp place that you got used to.

He was in San Diego when he mustered

70

out of the Navy and his first job had been in that town. He had gotten about seven thousand dollars in jewelry from a house and used it to travel back home. In hindsight, a stupid job. Not well thought out and not much to show for it, even though he hadn't been pinched. He began studying more after that. Coins being part of the study.

In Denver, he had taken the entire collection of coins from a guy who owned an insurance company. Liberty dimes minted in 1837 with no stars, fetching $2900 apiece; Standing Liberty quarters with stars under the eagles, valued at $13,000 per; Knobbed 6 half-dollars worth $5,600. Put a couple hundred in a sack and it added up. A fence had once given him seventy thousand dollars for eight coins that had been struck in France for its American colonies in the eighteenth century, pre-Revolution. A man could do well with coins.

Morning traffic in the Main Line. Minivans and SUVs running to schools, stopping by the local Starbucks afterward. The air cool and pleasant away from the city. A two-hour drive from Baltimore, yet a very different place.

The house where he would do the job was nice, but it was not ostentatious. This was not a real concern to Bridger. Not everyone with money showed it off. And there were people who lived in mansions without any furniture because they put all their earnings toward mortgage payments.

He drove by slowly, but not too slowly, and kept his cool when he saw the front door open. A woman came out. A good-looking woman with dark hair wearing a scarf around her skirt. The man's wife. Bridger put his eyes over the steering wheel and kept going. Got to the corner and turned.

For some reason, it made him think of Maggie.

Strange, that.

Bridger had been married before. While he was in the Navy. A girl he had gone with in high school. Her name was Donna. Came back from a ten-month tour and found that she had been sleeping with a buddy of his. They had all gone to school together. Bridger had slept with prostitutes in the Philippines and he was not going to throw stones. And the guy she had taken up with was pretty much a straight shooter; steady job at General Motors and so forth. Bridger asked her if she wanted a divorce. Donna got around to saying yes and he felt relieved. Sad, but relieved. He was not the same man who married her. He had been a boy then, really. And though his replacement was no prince, he was certainly no crook. His decision to let her go was an acceptance of the situation, of the sort of man he was.

He remained single after that. No wife, no kids. Women here and there, because he liked women and needed them. He understood that he was better suited to the Maggies than he was the Donnas.

But Maggie was something of a puzzle to him. Or, rather, made him feel like he was puzzled. Or weak. After her husband had died and they had started sleeping together, Bridger heard himself suggest that they move in together. He wanted her in his home. Not because he distrusted her; that was not his nature. He just wanted her around. Maggie said no. In fact, she would rarely even spend the night with him.

Last night in the storage room was, unfortunately, typical. A quick fuck in a storage room. It was the sort of thing she liked. Hurried, clothes partially on, dangerous. She told him she had trouble sleeping in other people's beds. That she could not get a full night's sleep if she stayed with him.

Which Bridger didn't really understand. He sometimes thought it was because she used to be a prostitute and it had fucked up her views on sex. Maybe for her, it had to be dirty and shameful. But then, he had known men who had married prostitutes, brought them back from the Philippines, and those women usually became very traditional wives and mothers. Sometimes to the degree that the sailors missed the exotic party girl they had married.

So what was it with Maggie? Why couldn't she make a home with him? He did not feel it was an unreasonable thing. She was a misfit, like him. They were good friends. It could work if she'd let it.

Bridger saw a small neighborhood coffee shop and pulled in. He parked the car and went inside. There was a line. Women, mostly. A man in hospital scrubs talking in a loud voice about how many surgeries he had to do that day, wanting other people to hear him. Bridger saw the woman when he got near the front.

Jesus. She was in the same line. The same woman he had seen ten minutes ago. Standing close enough to him that he could see the patterns on the scarf she had around her waist.

She looked even better up close. Nodding at people she knew, but not really engaging them in conversation. A quiet lady with a cool look about her.

Bridger took his eyes off her and ordered a small coffee. The cashier asked, for here? And he said, no, to go, because he had changed his mind.

He had had enough of black coffee in the Navy. He went to the condiment stand for the milk and sugar.

And heard a voice behind him ask if he could hand her a stir stick. He suspected it was her before he turned around and it was.

"Thank you," she said. And smiled at him.

"You're welcome," Bridger said.

"Lovely day, isn't it?"

"Yeah," Bridger said. "It's going to be nice." He smiled back because not smiling would have seemed unusual. "Take care," he said, and got the hell out of there.

NINE

When Russ Morrow had been a rookie working patrol, he was teamed up with a gray-haired Irish beat cop of the old school. The guy's name was Dunnigan and he was a walking cliché: gut hanging over the belt, possessed of a grizzly's strength, racist but compassionate, loud but subtle, temperamental and cynical, yet as maudlin as Tip O'Neil. Dunnigan said the brass would smile all they liked but at the end of the day they'd push you off a cliff. Dunnigan said Jimmy Breslin was a full of shit poser, but was right about the English. (As if Russ Morrow knew who he was talking about.) Dunnigan said Ronald Reagan was the dumbest fuck who ever sat in the White House and said only an Irishman could ever pull off going from *Bedtime for Bonzo* to the Presidency. (Which Russ Morrow didn't quite understand.) Dunnigan said that niggers made you feel sorry for the "good ones" and that women shouldn't be cops for reasons that were obvious, but that Morrow's generation would be wise to keep their thoughts to themselves on that subject if they wanted to rise above being a beat cop. Dunnigan said his time was past and he could give a shit what anyone did to him.

Dunnigan's standard line was: "Let me ask you something: can they take away my paycheck? Huh? Can they take away my paycheck? No? Then fuck 'em."

The answer, Russ would come to know, was, yes, they could take away your paycheck if you said the word "nigger" or if you said women had no business being cops and that this was not necessarily a bad thing. But that culture came in after Dunnigan retired and moved to upstate New York to drive his rural neighbors crazy.

Years passed since Russ Morrow was a smooth-faced rookie. Things change and they don't change.

What Russ Morrow was thinking about this morning was Dunnigan's comments on the FBI. An organization he hated more than Republicans and Democrats and Oliver Cromwell combined. Dunnigan said, "When an FBI agent demands something from you as if you're some sort of fucking field hand, the proper response is: fuck you."

Homicide Lieutenant Russ Morrow, with nineteen years of service behind him and one left to go before he could draw his pension, wished he could say that now.

He was sitting in a briefing room at the Philadelphia PD downtown headquarters with the Deputy Commissioner, Harold Blakely, and three feds. One of the feds was the Philadelphia FBI Section's SAC (Special Agent in Charge) and he wanted you to know it, too. The other two were guys in their thirties, one at the low end, the other at the high; both of them younger than Russ Morrow, one black and one white, both wearing Brooks Brothers suits.

Russ Morrow was not a bigot. But he was a lieutenant of some accomplishment and years of experience. And he had to sit quietly as the feds spoke to the Deputy Commissioner as if he were a simpleton, or, as if he were not there at all. The young black FBI agent sometimes shaking his head at the incompetence of the municipal police.

As Deputy Commissioner Blakely said, "I assure you, we're working every lead. And we hope to have a break soon."

The SAC said, "And who is leading this investigation?"

Blakely gestured to Russ Morrow. Morrow raised his hand, nudging an attitude.

The SAC made a point of sighing.

"Well," the SAC said, "what have you got?"

Lt. Morrow said, "I've got two dead people in a bodega. The black male is Termane Goode Jr. He was the one shot by the clerk. He had a firearm on him, but it had not been discharged. The clerk said there were two black males in the store. He can't remember much about the second one."

One of the younger agents, the white one named Sam Zabriskie, asked him, "What do you mean, he can't remember?"

Morrow said, "Did you read the report? His statement's in there."

"Why don't you tell me instead?"

Morrow leveled a glance at the younger man. Briefly, then went on.

"He said it happened very quickly. The second man went behind the aisle. He said that was all he saw of him because when he heard the shots he dropped to the ground and reached for his weapon."

"Was his firearm registered?"

"Yes." Morrow said, "For chrissake, he's a frightened old man. Do you want me to hardcase him?"

The black agent, whose name was Adam Roarke, said, "We're just concerned."

"About what?" Morrow said.

"That your compassion for this witness — which is understandable — has prevented you from getting the full story from him. He did, after all, kill a man."

Lt. Morrow said, "If you want me to interview him again, I'll be glad to do it. If you want to interview him yourself, be my guest."

Agent Zabriskie said, "We lost one of our agents. A man with a family. A law enforcement officer, like you. You can appreciate that, can't you?"

"Sure," Morrow said. "Look, we're working on it."

Zabriskie went on as if he wasn't listening. "That makes this a federal investigation. Do you see that?"

The Deputy Commissioner said, "We understand. You want our assistance, we'll give you as much as we can. But in order to do that, we need to know what your man was doing. What he was working on. It could be he was just in the wrong place at the wrong time. But . . . that's not the only possibility. If he was working undercover." The Deputy Commissioner said, "Was he?"

The SAC looked over to the other two agents. He nodded his assent and Special Agent Zabriskie said, "Yes. He was deep undercover in the Tessa crime family. He'd been in there for almost two years."

Morrow said, "Looking for what?"

"Anything," Roarke said. "We want to shut the family down. He was given free rein. Go in and watch."

Morrow said, "Did he ever give you any indication that they were onto him?"

After a moment, Zabriskie said, "No."

Morrow said, "Well, then. We're looking at a couple of possibilities. One, your man happened to be in a bodega when two guys went in with the intention of holding it up . . . but that doesn't really gibe with the clerk's statement. No one ever demanded money from him. No money was taken. The other possibility, the two men were sent after your man to kill him and it didn't go as planned."

The SAC said, "So where is the other man?"

"I don't know," Morrow said. "But I've got detectives checking out Termane Goode's associates. I think we'll track the second man down soon."

The SAC left them in the parking lot and the agents walked to their car. A cool, blue morning. Yellow cabs and buses moving down Market Street; commercial traffic only. Foreign tourists on their way to see the Liberty Bell.

The agents walked past Old City Hall.

It was Roarke who spoke first. He said, "How much should we disclose?"

Zabriskie said, "It depends. Right now, we give as much as is necessary."

"Need to know basis?" Roarke seemed uncertain.

"Yes."

Two men of different backgrounds. Roarke was a man from humble circumstances. Brooklyn born, law degree from Fordham University. He had placed his faith in education and had not regretted doing so. Before he decided on a career in the FBI, he had given serious consideration to the Marine Corps. He had been impressed with the recruiter from the Corps because the guy had seemed so *sure* about it all. While the Air Force recruiter had said things like "knock on wood" and so forth. Roarke was not unintelligent and he recognized that the Air Force recruiter was probably straighter than the Marine; yet he had been drawn to the Marine's confidence and presentation. Special Agent Roarke's suits were always clean and his shirts were always pressed.

Special Agent Sam Zabriskie was a Mormon. Born in Salt Lake City, his middle name was Norman, but he used it as little as possible because it rhymed and the jokes could get tiresome. Norman the Mormon. He had a preference for gray suits and white shirts. He awoke every morning at five A.M. so he could run three miles before work.

Zabriskie said, "John was a good agent. And I think he was getting close to Hannon. The people out here . . . it's not that I don't trust them. But . . . it's an old city with practices of corruption that perhaps haven't died out yet. Joe Hannon has friends in the Philadelphia Police Department. If we discuss it, now, with Lt. Morrow or his Commissioner, it could get back to him. And then John's work will have been in vain. You understand that, don't you?"

"I understand it," Roarke said.

But Zabriskie wasn't so sure Roarke did understand it. Zabriskie said, "It's important to be patient, Adam. We are something . . . more . . . than a mere law enforcement agency, you see. Part of our mission is to gather intelligence. People like Nick Blanco, the Tessa Family, they're not just criminals. They are a menace to our way of life. We have a duty to dismantle such organizations. To look at the bigger picture.

I think John would understand that, don't
you?"

"Yes, sir."

"Good."

Ten

By three o'clock he had worked it out.

He drove the Buick to a hotel in Valley Forge and parked it in the back lot. He checked in, paid cash and signed a false name. In the room, he brought a suit bag and his black attaché case.

He locked the door and chained it. He lay on the bed and stared up at the ceiling, closed his eyes and went to sleep.

Bridger left the room at one A.M., dressed in the black suit and carrying the attaché case. He put the clothes he was wearing earlier in the suitbag and put that in the trunk. He drove the car to the neighborhood near Drexel Hill, drove past the Hannon house. There were no lights on. He kept driving . . . two and a half miles away, where he parked the car in a shopping center lot. He left the car there, and began walking.

When he got to the house, it was two-thirty in the morning. It was a three-story white stone house built before the First World War, sitting up on a hill, the driveway going up and around the back. There was a garage back there with a Volvo station wagon inside. He checked the garage for toys and bicycles to see if there would be children in the house. There were no toys or bicycles. He cut the telephone wires.

When he got back to the back door, he saw a cat crouched on the step. Little black and white one staring up at him with yellow eyes. Not the problem a dog would present, cats could care less if you were robbing the house. But there was a little lion in each one of the little bastards and if they had another ninety pounds on them they'd go right for your throat and close the windpipe in their jaws with the same cold satisfaction they took in snuffing out birds and mice. Bridger had never liked cats, and he could smell one as soon as he stepped in a house.

"Get," he said.

The cat sprung away.

Bridger picked the lock instead of breaking it. He pulled the door open a crack, waited for a creak, didn't hear one and kept going. Then he was in and he shut the door behind him. He walked through a small utility room and into the kitchen. He took his

86

penlight out and turned it on. Copper pots and pans hanging near the stove, a large marble-topped island in the middle of the kitchen. A remodeled kitchen; probably had cost around forty thousand. Professionals living here. Old people did not spend money remodeling kitchens.

As he had in New York, he unlocked every door on the ground floor. He stood still and listened for a television or a radio. Signs of an insomniac. He didn't hear anything except the tick of a central heating system.

He climbed the stairs to the second story. There was another floor above that one and you would have to turn the corner to continue up a narrow set of stairs. When he reached the second level, he noticed something. There was no sound. That is, there was no sound of people sleeping. No breathing, no snoring.

What . . . ?

He turned to look up the staircase.

A bat came down on his head, before he could get his hand up to block it. Hit by another man wearing a ski mask. That was all he got sight of before he fell back, crying out, and then he was on the floor, reaching for the gun he had in his pocket, but the man was on top of him, grabbing him by his own mask, pulling his head up and slamming it back into the hard wood.

That was when he lost consciousness.

He was in Subic Bay and he knew it. Aware of himself in his Navy whites, flat hat, Chief Petty Officer Nagle saying this was the place to be, a nasty leer on his face. He had never liked Nagle. He was loud and obnoxious and not mature enough to be in a position of leadership. Airman ass, chief's mouth. Sailors sitting at a table playing happy face, a girl underneath the table doing dirty things to one of them, though not Bridger. He was aware that he was younger, yet also aware that he shouldn't be in this place, that he should have left this part of his life behind him by now. And then Maggie was standing next to the table saying, of all things, "How you doing, sailor?" No Philippine accent in her voice. Bridger said, "What are you doing here?" "Watching you, you naughty boy," she said. Maggie Chan of Baltimore in a place he had not known her. Maggie as he knew her, the age he knew her, yet wearing a black cocktail dress like all the whores. Bridger saying, "You shouldn't be here, Maggie." And she was smiling back at him . . . then not smiling, because she couldn't hold it anymore, a look of sorrow and fear on her face. And then

Bridger was saying, "Let's get out of here." Though not meaning to a hotel room or the backseat of a car, but out, to some other place . . . get out to escape because he was frightened . . . Maggie shaking her head now, saying, "I'm sorry, Danny. I'm sorry." Then fading away from him . . .

Dark when he opened his eyes. Dark, and then not so dark as things above him began to take shape. He was not in his house or a hotel room . . . the ceiling of a house.

He was laying on his back.

Wood floor.

He was at the bottom of the stairs.

Slowly, he got to his feet. The lights were still off. There was no sound. For a moment, he wondered if he had fallen down the stairs . . . no, he had been hit. It had been no hallucination. He looked down at the floor.

A .45 Glock near his foot.

He reached down to pick it up. His heart was pounding now and his instinct was to leave right away. But something was bothering him. He climbed back up the stairs, the gun in front of him now, keeping to the side of the wall.

When he reached the second story, he turned and pointed the gun up the second flight of stairs.

Nothing.

That was when he looked into the bed-room door.

Still dark in there. Two forms. Sleeping, right?

. . . oh, God.

He knew it, somehow he knew, before he switched on his penlight and approached the bed. And then he was standing over them and he knew he had to have more confirmation if only to retain his sanity. So he moved closer to them and switched on the bedside lamp.

When he did that, he knew the man and the woman were dead. Both of them shot several times, at least once in the head each.

He did not shout or scream, but a gasp escaped from his mouth that he could not control. And somehow, the thought that seemed to surface in that moment was, *Maggie, what have you done to me?* And whatever knowledge, whatever sureness he had ever had about anything in his life told him right then that there was no coin collection in this house. That there never had been.

He looked down at the gun he had in his hand. Then from the gun to the people in the bed.

Jesus, he had to get out of here.

He realized that he did not have his attaché case. And almost immediately decided that it did not matter, above all he had to get away from this place, get away from these deaths.

He moved down the stairs and went to the front door. It was still unlocked. He opened it and stepped out. He looked at his watch. Between four and five in the morning now, but still dark. He stepped off the front porch and got moving.

He kept away from the streets, and to the alleys. He felt the cold air on the wound on his head. It was sensitive to the touch — a little egg. But the blood had dried and it wasn't seeping. He still felt a little faint and he hoped he would not lose consciousness. With each step he told himself he would get better.

The first mile was uneventful. But then the tree-lined neighborhoods and alleys were behind him and he was in a more commercial area. He would have to go through some of this in order to reach the car, and with his head wound he was not sure he would have the stamina to make it. He would have to risk taking a bus or, worse, a cab. When he got to Darby Road, he did not see either one.

That was when he saw a squad car turn a

corner and start coming toward him. Slow-
ing as it approached.

Eleven

Bridger glanced at the patrol car as casually as he could. Four o'clock in the morning and there was nothing else to do but stand there. He still had the gun in his pocket. The same gun, probably, that had been used to kill the two people in the house, but he was in a bad place and he'd needed it when he left the house. Squad car approaching and he could take off running now or stand it out.

Under normal circumstances, it was better not to run. Run and they see a need to chase. You're just a man standing next to a street. Four in the morning, but you're just a man like any other. An insomniac, a night-shift worker, a homeless lunatic, a degenerate, a man taking a walk. Any of those things was more probable than a thief.

But these weren't normal circumstances. Someone had killed two people and set him up to answer for it. Someone had placed the murder weapon in his hand. Someone had wanted him to be there after it happened. Someone knew he would be.

The question was, had that someone placed an anonymous telephone call to the police? *I heard shots coming from a house.* Or, *there's a mysterious-looking man wearing a black suit wandering around the neighborhood.*

Bridger stared straight ahead, waiting for the patrol car to pass like it was a bus and he would walk across the street afterward.

The squad car passed by, Bridger catching a glimpse of blue uniform inside.

Bridger started to walk across the street.

He was halfway across and he could see the curb and the wet grass beyond, like it was an island.

And he heard the muffled whistle of depressed brakes as the police car slowed and began a slow U-turn.

Shit.

Bridger took off.

He heard the car accelerating now and then the siren was whooping and the blue and red lights were flashing and Bridger kept going, running all out now through the parking lot of a Burger King on the corner, running around the side with the drive-thru, past a car waiting and blocking passage for the police car. Ran past that and scaled a wood fence and got on the other side. Another parking lot and a fucking well-lit one at that. A convenience store with gasoline pumps in front. There was a Cadillac Seville with a guy starting to get in and Bridger pulled out the .45 and said "hey" and said, "Get away from that car." Still running while he said it and it disoriented the car's owner for a moment and then Bridger was next to the Cadillac and then behind the wheel and the key was in the ignition.

Bridger started the car and put it in gear as the police car was turning it into the parking lot of the convenience store and Bridger floored it and did a wide turn going out of the lot, heading west back toward the city.

The owner of the Cadillac stood back against the pumps as the police car squealed past him and made the same wide turn after the car thief and there was nothing for him to do then but watch his car fly away with the police car going after it, the siren diminishing in the distance.

Bridger glanced at the rearview mirror. Cherries flashing angrily, sirens screaming. He was driving east, pushing past seventy, moving away from the Main Line and closer to downtown and the river, driving in the middle of a black night, the police car's red and blue lights reflecting off the tree limbs that hung over the streets like the top of a cavern. There was very little traffic at this hour, but long car chases never ended well no matter how good you were and no matter how fast the car was because the police had radios and it only took a few minutes for other patrol units to come in like sharks on a bleeding quarry and helicopters with powerful spotlights putting you on the local television stations.

He was driving down a long stretch of road and coming to an intersection that met with another road like a half-crossed pair of scissors and he saw another police car, accelerating furiously on the other road and he knew that the men inside could see him as well as he could see them and they were ahead and would beat him to the intersection and cut him off.

But it was not that narrow a passage and Bridger let up on the gas and the police car shot out in front of the intersection, trying to block him, and Bridger guided the Cadillac to the left, the car skidding, but holding as it went around the backside of the police car. Bridger kept going and saw in the rearview that the chase car would not take the same chance as it braked hard and slid to a stop in front of the car blocking the intersection. Maybe colliding, maybe not, but they were stopped for the time being as Bridger kept the accelerator down and kept going.

He reached an entrance ramp to Interstate 76 and cut off another car, forcing it to a screeching stop as Bridger took the other's place in line and shot up the incline and went around another car when there really shouldn't have been enough room, but he got it past as metal screeched against metal and sparks flicked off in the darkness and Bridger put the car behind him.

And then he was on the interstate, the Schuykill Expressway, going about seventy-five now, but not much more because he did not want to attract more attention than he needed to.

He was moving south now, toward Center City. A couple of minutes passed and the river was on his left with the gingerbread boat houses on the other side. The art museum was coming into view now and in the distance, back but close enough, he saw the flicker of flashing lights. Christ. They were on the interstate now. Bridger floored it and saw an eighteen-wheel truck up ahead. He kept going until he passed it.

Then he maneuvered the car in front of the semi and lifted his foot off the gas. They would not be able to see him with the truck behind him. He kept it there for about a mile and peeled off the next exit, switching his lights off as he did so, the car descending down an exit ramp near Chestnut Avenue.

He had the Caddy underneath the interstate when the patrol car zoomed by above him, lights still flashing.

Better off now than he was five minutes ago, but he needed to ditch the car right away.

He parked it under a viaduct across the river from the art museum, walked three blocks, and found what he was looking for. The subway. When he got down the stairs he put his jacket and his tie into a trash can. He put the gun into a different trash receptacle.

Now he was a man wearing dark slacks and a white dress shirt. Cary Grant casual, but not fitting in a Philadelphia subway station. He saw a homeless man sitting on a bench with a shopping cart, aluminum cans in the cart.

Bridger went up to the guy.

"Hey," Bridger said. He showed the guy a wad of bills. "I'll give you two hundred bucks for your hat and coat."

"Two hundred? Let me see it."

"It's right here." Bridger told himself there was no need to get impatient with the man. He needed him and that was the way it was. "See? Come on," Bridger said, "help a brother out."

A moment passed and the man said, "All right. But no one's gonna believe it."

"Keep it to yourself," Bridger said, putting on the coat. "That way, no one will take it."

The homeless man had the money in his pocket by the time Bridger got on the next train.

TWELVE

When he got back to Baltimore, he went to his unregistered garage. The Nova was there and it gave him some comfort to see it. Something familiar. He had left the Buick in Philadelphia. It was not registered in his name and could not be traced back to him. He would consider it a loss at this point.

He slept on a cot in the garage for two hours. There were some things he needed to think about, but he could not think about them now because the exhaustion and the fear and the adrenalin would make it difficult to think clearly. He would have to think later and he would be safe in this garage. And as he lay down, he reminded himself that Maggie did not know where this garage was.

Woke up two hours later and thought, *I think she doesn't.* But what if she did? What had she gotten him into?

He wanted to believe that what had happened in Philadelphia was a coincidence. He just happened to break into a home shortly after the owners had been murdered. Bad timing, right?

No, that didn't make sense. He had based his jobs on what made sense. Time, place, setting. This didn't make sense. Besides, it was wishful thinking. Wishful to think that he just happened to be at the wrong place at the wrong time. Wishful thinking would put you in jail. And it didn't square with someone putting a murder weapon in his hand.

And not just any weapon. A .45 semiautomatic, the gun he favored.

So . . . fuck, someone had known that he would be there. Not just a thief, but one named Daniel Bridger.

He took another gun, a .38 snub, which was hidden in a milk carton in the refrigerator. He drove the Nova to her apartment on Charles Street. Drove past it and saw that her light was off. He parked near the Belvedere Hotel and walked back.

He walked up the three flights of stairs. Knocked on her door lightly. No answer. He picked the lock and got in.

The first thing he noticed was that the window was open. He could feel the draft from outside and hear the traffic going north. And in a way, he knew it then. Knew what he would find. Yet when he saw her face down on the kitchen floor, he still said, "Oh, no. Maggie."

He turned her over and saw the red stripe across her neck. She had been garroted. Murdered quietly. Brutally.

He knew he couldn't stay. Probably, they had been expecting him to come here. Counting on it.

Bridger went out the back door, his hand on the gun in his pocket. He didn't see anyone and he didn't run back to his car, but walked. It wasn't until he was in the car that he lost it. He had not wept since childhood.

THIRTEEN

Captain Hodges took another donut out of the Winchell's box that had been brought in that morning and set next to the coffeepot in the detectives' squad room. It was his third one this morning. He was a big man, Captain Hodges, like Dunnigan had been. But not like Dunnigan in spirit. Not as far as Russ Morrow was concerned. There was well over two-hundred-fifty pounds on Hodges's relatively small frame, and Morrow wondered if he'd live the few years he had left to get his pension.

Captain Hodges said, "It didn't happen in the city limits. Besides, he was a state judge. A public official. So it's PSP's jurisdiction."

PSP meant Pennsylvania State Police. The state agency that patrolled the state highways from Scranton to Pittsburgh. But they had their plainclothes detectives as well, investigating the murders of state public officials and helping out small towns with murder cases that went beyond domestic squabbles that got out of hand. The PSP also conducted criminal investigations on cops suspected of criminal activity when it became necessary.

Morrow said, "Do they want assistance from us? A joint task force?"

Hodges said, "Haven't been advised of such yet. We got a copy of the initial crime report from the local county police. Faxed this morning. Take a look at it sometime today, see if you can help."

"Did you read it?"

"Yeah, I read it. I tell you, it's a heck of a mess. Shot in their beds. An anonymous call placed to the local 911 that night, someone saying they'd heard gunshots. A man, white male in his thirties or forties, spotted by a county deputy about a mile from the house. The guy ran, stole a car. Got away. They think that's the man."

"A hit?"

"Maybe. Who knows at this point?"

Morrow said, "I testified in his court once."

"Judge Hannon's?"

"Yeah."

"Never met the man. What was he like?"

Morrow shrugged. "He was a nice guy, I guess. A politician."

That was the only time Morrow had seen the judge. In a judge-type setting. The man wearing black robes and sitting in a judge's pose behind the bench. Looking thoughtful and wise. But it was hard to see the man in that situation. A judge in his judge uniform, playing a role that he needed to play. But still a man underneath, with frailties and weaknesses like any other. Morrow had read the story about the judge in Oklahoma that was caught sticking his wanker in a penis pump under the bench. *During* trials. They took the black robe away from that one.

"Well," Hodges said, "the theory is that it's just a home invasion. But there are other possibilities."

They had taken the bodies away by noon, but the crime scene team was still upstairs, taking photos and swabs and things out of the carpet. They didn't want people using the telephones in the house or, for that matter, sitting on the furniture until they were finished.

The two detectives from the State Police were called Troopers even though they weren't wearing trooper hats or boots. They were dressed in dark, somber suits they got from Penneys and their black shoes were shined. They said they could ask their questions at Troop K headquarters at 2201 Belmont Avenue, which they would prefer, or they could do it at the kitchen table if that was her preference. Claire Laval said she preferred to remain in her home.

The troopers' names were Ronald Lytle and Harold Pierce. Both big men, Lytle looking like he had been in the military at one time, though he hadn't, Pierce with an outdated haircut and thick eyeglasses.

They sat at the kitchen table, Claire dabbing her eyes with a paper napkin here and there, a hot cup of coffee in front of her. It was the first thing she had done when she got home, made coffee. It seemed the thing to do.

Trooper Lytle said, "Ma'am, we're probably going to ask you questions you've already answered. I'm sorry about that."

"It's okay."

Lytle said, "To start with, my understanding is, the Montgomery Sheriff's office is the agency that notified you, correct?"

"That's right."

"On your cell phone?"

"Yes."

"And you were in New York?"

"Yes."

Lytle hesitated, being diplomatic. "Up there on business?"

"No. I was visiting a friend. Her name is Grace Appleton. She was a friend from college. My roommate. She and her sisters have a girls' weekend every year."

"Her sisters . . . ?"

"Well, they include me."

"And you stayed with her?"

"Yes."

"The whole time?"

Claire Laval looked up from her paper napkin. First at Lytle, then at Pierce. "Yes," she said. "You can call her if you like."

"Okay," Lytle said. "What's her number?"

Claire gave it to them. Pierce was the one who wrote it down.

Lytle said, "The woman who was found with your husband, her name is, was, Katherine Dunphy. Do you know her?"

"No."

"Are you sure?"

"Did you ever suspect your husband was seeing her?"

"No."

"Did you ever suspect that your husband was having an affair? With anyone?"

"No, but —"

"No, but what?"

Claire sighed, but she held on. It was unreal, all of it. Unreal. She said, "No, but I'm not that surprised."

"What do you mean by that?" Lytle caught the woman's hard glance then, and he said, "I mean, were there signs?"

"Well . . . yes and no. No, I never smelled perfume on him or anything. But we had been drifting apart for the last couple of years. I'm just saying I'm not that surprised."

"Are you angry with him?"

She gave him another look. Not anger, so much. But a direct look that made the police officers see her in a different light. "Well, detective, I just found out in one day that my husband was unfaithful to me and that he's been murdered. He was my husband. What am I supposed to feel? Is the sin he committed in life supposed to even out the horror of his death?"

Trooper Pierce said, "No, ma'am. We don't doubt that your grief is genuine. We're just doing our jobs."

"Well, I'm not the sort that condones murdering unfaithful men."

Lytle said, "No one has said that you are, ma'am. If you want to do this at a different time, we can do that."

"No, I'd prefer to finish it now."

Lytle said, "Did your husband have enemies?"

Claire was tired. Very tired. She said, "He

108

was a judge. He sent people to prison. I don't know. He never told me about any threats he received."

"Did he seem . . . agitated or anxious about anything?"

"I don't think so . . . well, perhaps. But about what, I have no idea. It may have been about the affair he was having."

Lytle said, "Anything else you can think of?"

"No. I can't think of anything else that would be bothering him. We didn't — we didn't talk that much the last few months. I mean, we talked, but we didn't talk. He would say the right things to me, show the right facial expressions of interest and concern when I talked to him." She smiled, half in regret. "He was good at that. He was a good politician. But I knew him well enough to know he wasn't that interested."

Lytle said, "How did you know?"

"I just . . . did."

"And you were okay with that?"

"Okay with what?"

"Okay with this . . . distance in your marriage?"

After a moment, Claire Laval said, "I don't know. What difference does it make now?"

Trooper Lytle said, "I guess not much."

He looked to the other detective to see if there was anything else he should ask. Trooper Pierce shook his head, and Lytle turned back to the widow.

"Mrs. Hannon, we don't have any other questions at this time. I'm going leave you my card. Call me anytime if you want to talk about anything. If you think of anything else we should be looking into. It's a homicide investigation. We're confident that we'll catch the man that did this. I'll keep in touch with you, keep you apprised."

Claire said, "You have a suspect?"

"Well," Lytle said, "we have a lead. We think what happened here was a home invasion. We believe a burglar broke in to steal and found your husband and Miss Dunphy and, maybe panicked, and shot them both."

Claire said, "What about the woman? Did she have a husband?"

"No," Lytle said. "No boyfriend either. She was an attorney. We're checking that out too, but we do not believe this was connected to her."

"Why do you think it was a burglar?"

"The police were called last night around three A.M. by someone who said they heard gunshots coming from your home. Within an hour, a man was seen walking in the street about a mile from here. A patrol officer stopped to question him and the man ran. He pointed a pistol at a man in a convenience store parking lot and stole the man's car. He got away. Now, that could just be a coincidence, but we doubt that it is. We think it's the same man that killed your husband. We think it's the same man that was trying to rob this house."

Claire said, "He got away?"

"Yes. I'm sorry."

"What did he look like?"

Lytle turned to Pierce again. Pierce said, "White male, taller and bigger than average. Between thirty-five and forty-five. He was wearing dark clothing, a black suit and a white shirt. That's all we have now."

Lytle said, "Does it sound like anyone you know?"

Claire Laval said, "It could be any number of people I know. That's a very broad description. I don't know people who break into people's homes and steal. Don't you have — don't you have anything more than that to go on?"

"No, ma'am, not at this time," Lytle said. "But it's early in the investigation. We will produce something, I promise you."

Claire said, "How did he get away?"

"He just . . . stole a car and got away. I'm sorry, it happens."

"Is he going to come back here?"

Lytle said, "Come back here? For what?"

"To kill me?"

"I don't see why he would," Trooper Lytle said. "Look, you have my number. I wrote my personal cell number on there too. If you need anything, you can call me anytime. Okay?"

Claire saw the ring on the man's third finger and he saw that she saw because he pulled his hand back, just before catching himself.

Shit, Claire thought. Because she knew something about men. She did not want to think this about this man. Not after the death of her husband, not after the detective had been sent here to help her, to help solve the crime. But she knew, even if he did not, that the detective was hoping to get a little nookie out of this. There, there, Mrs. Hannon. There, there. Calling her Mrs. Hannon as if he knew her, when everyone who knew her knew she had never taken Joe's name. She hoped she was wrong in drawing this conclusion, but she was too tired to hope about it right now.

"Okay," she said. She looked at the other detective, the one named Pierce who had mostly kept to himself and taken notes. She said, "Do you have a card too?"

She saw Trooper Lytle's face fall, just a bit, as Trooper Pierce took a card from his wallet and slid it over to her. He did not write his cell number on his card.

FOURTEEN

Nick Blanco's house was one of those three-story Georgians with windows spaced evenly on all floors. He had married a woman named Lacey Manahan who had red hair and clear, pale skin and who had expensive taste. It was Lacey who picked the house out, Lacey who dealt with the real estate people so that they would not know they were dealing with a gangster. Nick paid a good price for the house and then matched the asking price with improvements to it. One hundred fifty thousand went to rewiring alone before they even talked about furniture and building the back deck. Nick Blanco was conscious that men under him were watching these events to see if he was the sort of man who let broads push him around. So when Lacey came to him and requested both a tennis court *and* a swimming pool, he said she could have one or the other, but not both. One of his few victories.

On this day, as he saw her come off the tennis court in her white skirt and v-necked shirt, he told himself it was worth it. Tight little ass filling out the skirt just so, breasts firm but not too big. Not as big as Angie's, his first wife. Angie who had been a cute girl at twenty with big tits and then ballooned somewhere around thirty. Nick got involved with Lacey somewhere around then, bought her presents: two-thousand-dollar handbags, diamond earrings, and such until Angie confronted him about it and he responded by telling her he was going out for cigarettes and never coming back.

The Tessa family had not been happy with him for leaving Angie. Old school guys who still wanted to live in another century but couldn't tell you why. Giving him shit because he had dumped an Italian girl from South Philly for a skinny bitch who thought she was some sort of Katherine Hepburn. Like Angie had been their little sister or something. *Well,* Nick thought, *fuck 'em.* He made money for the Tessas. He oversaw heroin sales and marketing for them in Philadelphia and produced millions in profit for them. He had given them plenty. So as far as he was concerned, who he wanted to

115

make his wife was his business. He knew it and they knew it too, so they could bitch, but they wouldn't push him too hard on the subject.

But, Christ, it could be a nuisance. What it came down to was, Nick Blanco wasn't guinea enough for them. Guilty of acting like a WASP. Never mind that Lacey Manahan was a Catholic girl who went to mass every Sunday. That wasn't good enough to satisfy the Tessas. What they wanted him to do was stay with Angie or a girl like Angie. Dumb, unsophisticated girl, who would say "fuck" in restaurants loud enough so people would turn and look. A girl like that. Lacey would say it too, though it seemed different when she did. And she had never embarrassed him in public.

He was vaguely aware that he would be cut more slack if he lived the way they wanted him to. Say, if he lived in a brownstone in South Philly and had a big stomach and wore cheap knit shirts and kept a big cigar in his mouth. Maybe then they wouldn't be so eager to breathe down his neck when they found out there was an FBI agent that had infiltrated the Family.

He felt a little better today. Today, the guinea fucks should be satisfied. He had gotten rid of the fed, which they knew about, and he had gotten rid of Joe Hannon, which they had not. And he had taken care of the Chinese woman himself.

That had not been difficult. He had known Maggie back when she was McGurn's wife. He did not dislike her and he understood what had drawn McGurn to her. He had not enjoyed killing her. It had been years since he had killed a woman. But to his way of thinking, Maggie Chan had made a conscious decision to get into this life once she took up with Jack McGurn. And she had made another conscious decision to stay in this life when she took up with Dan Bridger after her husband was dead. As with her husband, it had been nothing personal. Just a necessary task.

He smiled at his wife as she walked up to the table on the back deck, her friend Laura walking behind her. Laura was another country club beauty. Nick liked having women like that around. He never made a play for them, but he liked having them around.

Lacey kissed him on the mouth. Showing him off a bit, kissing her good-looking husband in front of Laura.

Lacey said, "Laura beat me. I think we need to hire a tennis pro."

"Sure," Nick said. "What's her name?"

"*His* name would be Jimmy or Lester. About twenty years old with blond hair. Laura recommends him highly."

"Don't tease me," Nick said. "I'm not a young man anymore."

But he liked that his wife would say such things to him. She flattered him often because she knew he liked it. But she meant what she said. He was a handsome man who kept his stomach flat. And he was not a bad tennis player himself.

"Young in spirit," Laura said. "That's what counts."

Yes, a very pleasant morning. Cool and sunny with warmer weather on the way. A man being flattered by two beautiful, classy women. *Town and Country* women. And then the phone rang and he wished he'd left it alone. The phone sitting on the table, clanging into their conversation.

Nick said, "I got it."

Claude Maddox said, "I need to see you."

Nick said, "Why?" His voice firm, telling the man it better be important.

"Problems," Maddox said. "It's not something we should wait on, Nick."

An hour later, Nick Blanco was in the back room of a barber shop with dirty floors and the smell of old men and tonic, Hispanic music drifting in from down the street because the spics always had to play that shit full blast. Back in South Philly. Claude Maddox was not the sort that kept bad news to himself. Not the sort to keep something from Nick. He said, "If you're angry with me, I understand it. But you've got to admit, it was an honest mistake. And we were working on short notice."

Kenny D was leaning against the wall, his arms folded. He looked at the floor and he didn't say anything.

Nick said, "I'm not mad at you, Claude. I just — don't see how this could happen."

"Look, I've never seen the man's wife before, all right? I went in and I presumed the woman in bed with him was his wife. I didn't know the man had a girlfriend. Vince never told us that, right?" Maddox changed his tone. "I mean, he never told me."

Nick Blanco looked at Maddox for a moment and wondered if there was something of a challenge there. "No," Nick said, "he never told me, either. But, Christ, Claude, you should have checked that out."

"Nick, there wasn't time. We did all these things on short notice. I mean, what I'm saying is, we did everything as planned. Kenny made the anonymous call and told the police he heard the shots, I took care of

Hannon and the woman in bed with him. And we got rid of the black guys."

"But, Claude, this is the sort of thing we can't do at ninety percent. Right?"

"The fed was working Judge Hannon, not his wife."

"Right, but we're talking about the man's wife here. Besides, it's her restaurant, see? It was her restaurant that we were running the money through. You think she didn't know about it?"

"I don't know what she knew. Or knows."

"I'm not saying I do either, Claude. I can't know everything. But the odds are, she knows. And we can't have that."

"All right, then," Maddox said. "You want me take care of her, I'll take care of her. But it's gonna mess things up. You can pin the judge's murder on Bridger, but how are you gonna pin the wife on him too?"

"I don't know. I'll think of something. But it's going to have to be done, even if it is messy. We can sit here and hope, or we can be sure. You agree with me that it's better to be sure?"

Maddox looked at Kenny D, who looked back at him and nodded. "All right," Maddox said. "I'm down with that."

FIFTEEN

For as long as Adam Roarke had known Zabriskie, he had never seen the man drink a caffeinated beverage. Not once. No Coke, no coffee, no Diet Pepsi. Sam Zabriskie did not even drink decaffeinated coffee. The only thing you would ever find in Sam's coffee cup was water. Other agents said that Sam was a mix of that agent Smith from *The Matrix* and Ned Flanders. Pop culture references that were lost on Sam because he did not watch television or films. Nor did he own a DVD player. Adam believed you could put Sam Zabriskie in a time machine and send him back to the fifties or send him a century into the future and his appearance and his expression and his way of life would remain exactly the same. Had he been an agent under the authority of J. Edgar Hoover, he would have obeyed orders to tape record all of Martin Luther King's extramarital affairs and done so without question and without the slightest hesitation. And in a different time and in a different place, he would have obeyed orders to build the strongest case possible against a police officer accused of violating an African American's civil rights. With the same dedication.

Sam Zabriskie sat in his office behind his desk. He was in his white shirt sleeves; it was only when he was in his office that he removed his jacket.

Adam Roarke leaned against the door to Sam's office. He had shut it behind him after he came in.

Sam Zabriskie looked at a preliminary police report that appeared on his screen. He clicked the computer's mouse a couple of times and then there was the *Philadelphia Inquirer*'s website story about the Hannon murder. To Roarke, he did not seem particularly perturbed about anything he saw on the screen. But then, Roarke thought, Sam never seemed particularly perturbed about anything.

After reading the stories on the computer screen, Sam turned to acknowledge the younger agent.

"Okay," Sam said. Finished with his review. "Well, as he was a state judge, the matter will be assigned to the Pennsylvania

State Police."

Roarke waited for him to say something else. He didn't.

Roarke said, "Is there anything else?"

"What do you mean?" Sam said.

"I mean, don't you think there's something else we should be concerned about?"

"No. It's not our jurisdiction."

"I understand that, but . . . Sam, that's not . . ."

"That's not what?"

"That's not the issue."

Sam Zabriskie stared at the younger agent briefly, a passive expression on his face. A patient man, he was. Sam said, "I'm not following you."

Roarke said, "We were building a case against Hannon."

"Yes." Like, go on.

"Well, I think it's a factor in the investigation."

Sam said, "Our investigation is over. Joseph Hannon is dead. It's moot, Adam."

"I understand that Hannon was the target of our investigation. But now there's a murder investigation."

"But that's not ours. It's not ours to investigate."

"Isn't it? Obviously, Nick Blanco was behind it."

"We don't know that."

"We don't know, but we *know*. John is killed, then the very next day, Judge Hannon is killed. That's not a coincidence. In fact, it's A, B, C. Blanco found out about John and Judge Hannon and had them whacked. Blanco knew."

Sam Zabriskie seemed to think about it. Seemed to think about a point that, to Roarke, was so elementary that any regular viewer of a cop television show would put it together ten minutes after the opening theme music. Yet Sam sat there and frowned like it was something novel and interesting, but not terribly solid. It was an act and it was pissing Adam Roarke off.

Finally, Sam said, "It's a theory, Adam. I'll acknowledge that it's a reasonable theory. But it's not evidence."

"It's not *direct* evidence. But you know — I mean, we know, that we rarely get direct evidence in cases like this. There's not going to be a videotape of the killings, an audiotape of the discussions that went on before and after. It's *circumstantial* evidence, but people are convicted on that."

"Adam . . ." Sam's tone was one of disappointment, because he could see what was coming. Could see it when Adam had walked in his office and kept his back to the door like they were sneaking cigarettes in the bathroom. Could see that the younger agent was scared.

"We should have told the Philly PD," Roarke said. "We should have said something yesterday."

"Adam, listen to me. We didn't know anything yesterday. How could we know that this was going to happen?"

"We should have known."

"No. Joe Hannon should have known. He should have known you can't make bargains with the devil. That was his choice, not ours."

Adam Roarke looked at the senior agent for a moment. He did not know how to respond to that one.

Sam said, "Besides, what do you suggest we do now? Go tell Lieutenant Morrow of the Philadelphia Police Department that we were investigating one of their judges for corruption? Do you think they would appreciate that?"

"I do, actually. And it's not Philly PD's case. It's the state police's."

"Well, then. There you are."

It occurred to Adam Roarke then, perhaps for the first time, that Sam was one of those people who had the gift of being able to speak with such confidence and presence that you were tempted to believe he was right even when you knew what he was saying was wrong. It was not that he spoke with passion. Not hardly. But such precision and sureness. It explained, in part, his success at the Agency. It was a sureness so firm that it made Roarke hesitate and even doubt himself.

Sam said, "Adam. I understand your concern. I do. In fact, I admire it. You're a conscientious agent and a good one. But you are not obligated to accept responsibility for things beyond your control. These things happen, but it does not mean you're at fault. Or that we're at fault. As I said a moment ago, Joe Hannon is responsible for Joe Hannon. We did not push him into associating with Nick Blanco or anyone else. That was his decision."

"But there is a murder investigation."

"Of course. And what will they say to us if we tell them? If we tell them what we know? That we got him killed? That we stuck our noses where they didn't belong? That we're trying to interfere with their investigation? What will be gained by that?"

Roarke thought, what would be gained is he would feel better. Would be able to sleep better at night knowing he had not hidden things he should not be hiding. But how do you tell that to this man?

"I don't know," Roarke said.

"All right," Sam said. "How about this: let's at least not do anything for a couple of days. The reports say that Judge Hannon was with a woman who wasn't his wife. It's just as likely that that got him killed as much as anything. Certainly, that theory is as plausible as yours. Don't you agree?"

"Well . . ."

"Considering that, if we speak up now, we could well be *interfering* with the State's investigation. And that's not going to benefit anyone. So why not be patient for a couple of days?"

Agent Roarke looked at the floor for a while. Then said, "If you think it's best."

"I do." Sam stood up and walked to the door. He took his gray jacket off a wood hanger and began to slip it on. He said, "Did you get the memo this morning?"

"Which one?"

"Congress wants all field offices to assign more agents to investigating pornography. There's a meeting in Mel's office in ten minutes. We're all supposed to review the directive together."

They were moving down the hallway before Roarke could say anything more about the Hannon issue. As they got to the conference room, Roarke asked, "Are they cracking down on child pornography?"

"No," Sam said, "the adult kind."

Sixteen

"Pennsylvania State Police, Troop K. How may I help you?"

"Trooper Ronald Lytle, please."

"Who may I say is calling?"

"A friend."

"And what is it regarding?"

"The Hannon murder investigation," Kenny D said. "I got something that may help him with his investigation."

There was a pause. "We need to know your name, sir."

"No you don't. Tell him I know who killed the judge. Tell him I'm counting to twenty and then I'm getting off this phone."

Kenny D was using a pay phone at the I-76 rest stop in Valley Forge. Standing among a bustling crowd moving in and out of public restrooms, getting in line for the Wendy's takeout, the smell of hamburger grease mingling with floor cleaner.

About fifteen seconds passed and there

was another voice on the line.

"Lytle speaking."

"You the man that was in the paper? The one investigating the Hannon murder?"

"I am. Who are you?"

"A friend. Your man is a thief named Daniel Bridger of Baltimore, Maryland. B-R-I-D-G-E-R. Write it down. Or play your tape back after I hang up."

"Who is this?"

"Check him out," Kenny said. "See if he matches the description of the guy the cops let steal a car and get away. Betcha a Coke he does."

"Who —"

Kenny hung up the phone.

At least fifteen minutes passed by before they could get a unit to the rest stop. A good fourteen minutes after Kenny D left, his car slipping into the daily traffic of the interstate.

SEVENTEEN

Bridger didn't say much to Sonny that day at the garage. Neither one of them was talkative by nature, but today he barely said anything to the man. Sonny was not the sort to pry, but when that half-hour stretch between four-thirty and five came and the day slowed down, Bridger told him that Maggie was dead.

"What happened?" Sonny said.

"Someone murdered her."

Sonny had not ever expressed an emotion one way or another about Maggie. But he knew she meant something to Bridger. He asked, "Do you know who?"

"No."

"Do the police know?"

"I don't know. I doubt it."

"Have you asked them?"

"No."

There was a silence then. And Sonny somehow knew not to ask anything else. He said, "That's bad. I'm sorry, Dan."

Bridger wiped some excess gunk off a socket wrench. "Yeah, it's bad," he said. He thought about adding something. Something like, "but it's not over." But it would sound stupid. He had no need to impress Sonny. Nor did he want to. Besides, truth be told, he was not sure what to do. Not yet, anyway. Last night, he had found a woman who he cared for strangled to death, and this morning he had come to work. On time. He had not gotten drunk. He had not made any arrangements for burial. He had not said a prayer. He had not done anything. He felt a little unclean about it. *A woman you cared for is murdered and you just go back to work. What sort of man does that?* He could remind himself, again, that the police would probably blame him for it. That Maggie had obviously mixed the both of them up in something. He could tell himself that, but it didn't mean anything. Didn't excuse just going back to work.

Sonny said, "Maybe you not come in tomorrow."

"Yeah, maybe."

He cleaned up and got in his Nova and drove north on Falls Road. He went past the rowhouses of the Hampden neighborhood and continued past the Cross Keys shopping center. Going home to a house that he had always lived alone in, yet, perhaps for the first time, worrying about sitting alone in his house. Turn the television on, cook dinner to the sound of it, continuing life as he always had, yet it would be different. Feeling anxious, yet tired too. And then he realized he did not want to cook this evening.

He stopped at a convenience store in the Mount Washington neighborhood, near the Jones Falls Expressway. He picked up a prepackaged sandwich and put it in the store's microwave. He had done worse. When it dinged that it was done, he pulled it out and placed it between a handful of white napkins. He took a six-pack of 8-ounce Coke — the little bottles — from the shelf and was rounding the corner of an aisle when he saw the cop standing in front of the sales counter.

A young one with a chubby face and novice smile. He was making small talk with the clerk. Something about how you were better off taking the train to the Orioles games because the cost of parking was so freaking high. The sort of cop that took care not to use foul language in front of non-criminals.

He looked directly at Bridger as he came

to the counter. "How you doing?" Friendly.

"Fine," Bridger said.

Bridger thought, don't get paranoid. You can't go through life avoiding every policeman you see. There were too many. And he was not in Philadelphia anymore, so it shouldn't matter.

It was a rational way to think about things. But . . . he noticed that the police officer rested his eyes on him a little longer than normal. Then he noticed the officer looking out the window at Bridger's Nova.

Then the cop stopped looking at him. Made a point of it, in fact. And returned his attention to the clerk.

"Yeah," the cop said, "they could use some pitching though."

The Orioles, he meant. But he hadn't been talking about their game. He had been talking about the difficulty of getting a decent parking space at Camden Yards. And had his body language changed? The cop looked over at Bridger. Bridger gave him a half smile. Right? Right.

Bridger paid for his things and left.

He was pulling out of the parking lot when his cell phone rang. He took it out of his pocket and saw that it was Sonny calling from the garage.

"Yeah?"

"Danny, the police just left here. They're looking for you. Are you going home?"

After a moment, Bridger said, "I was."

"They seem pretty mad about something. I think they on their way to you house. Just thought I'd tell you."

"Thanks. I wouldn't worry about it too much, Sonny. Later."

He clicked the phone off and threw it out the window. Saw it smash into pieces on the street in his rearview mirror. Cell phones could track you like a GPS if you weren't careful. They had caught other criminals that way.

Bridger turned north on Charles Street, took it to the beltway and took that to the airport. He left the Nova in the long-term parking garage and drove out in a big Mercury Marauder with Virginia tags. He replaced the tags with a set of Pennsylvanians he picked up from his non-registered garage, the one he didn't share with Sonny. The police would not know about this one, but he felt better when he got out of there with another .45 and five thousand dollars he had kept hidden in the icebox. It looked like he was going back to Philly after all.

EIGHTEEN

It was the part after the funeral that was the worst. People coming up to her and telling her what a good man Joe had been. Adding things like, "you know." Like, considering. You know. Yeah, they knew. Who could not know? It had been in all the newspapers, on all the television stations. *Judge murdered in bed with his mistress.* People telling her she was a saint. Like it was supposed to make her feel better. It didn't. Not in the slightest. Claire Laval never had any interest in being a saint. That role did not suit her. They were Catholics, most of his family. Irish Catholics. She was French Catholic, whatever that meant, but had never fit in with the Hannon tribe. Joe's mother saying, again and again, that her son was a good man. Defiantly. As if daring Claire to contradict her.

The family gathered at Joe's parents' house, not Claire's. And that was a relief.

That was a considerable relief. Because Claire was not sure she could have endured it if she thought some of these people would be staying in her home for the night. She vacillated between contempt for them and contempt for herself. The woman has lost a son, she would remind herself. And no person should have to bury one of their children. Not even Peggy Hannon. His father, thank God, had passed away years ago.

A white-haired man that Claire believed was an uncle of Joe's kept saying to her, "Three things, Claire. Three things: faith, family, and friends." Claire could smell whiskey on his breath, his words slurring. Claire said, "Thank you. I know. Thank you." She didn't know what else to say.

Peggy Hannon barely said a word to her. And it didn't take Claire long to figure that shit out. In the mother's mind, it had been Claire's fault. At least, partially. Had Claire kept her little Joe happy in the marriage, happy in the bedroom, he would not have taken up with another woman. Would not have been murdered. It was not remotely rational, but even Claire on this day could not feel anger at the woman. She had lost her son and to see her now was to understand the expression sick with grief.

137

When it became late evening, she embraced her mother-in-law, then made her way to the door. She was in the foyer putting her coat on when she realized the old uncle who spoke of faith, family, and friends was standing near her. She looked at him and remembered his name. Kevin, a cousin once removed. He reminded her a bit of Pat Moynihan. He looked back at her now and said, "Claire."

"Yes."

"Try not to hate him. Forgive him, okay? For your own sake, huh?"

She moved over to him and kissed him on the cheek. "I will," she said. "Thank you."

She cried almost all of the drive back home. Cried for Joe, cried for his mother, cried for Cousin Kevin. She cried because she was ashamed. Ashamed for feeling ugly thoughts about her husband's family members. She wondered if she was, at root, a cruel-natured person. Peggy's contempt for her was, perhaps, not excusable. But what was *her* excuse? She had always known that Peg Hannon was a foolish bitch and at times a holy terror. But that was Peggy's problem, not hers. Her husband had become something of a stranger. Her husband had become someone that, perhaps, she did not really know. Her husband had been fucking another woman in her bed. So what if all that was true? Was it any business of Joe's family? What harm was there in letting them grieve for a person they believed he was? Did she have a right to take that away from them? Maybe Peggy was justified in holding her responsible.

When she walked in the door of her home, her phone was ringing. Claire left it alone. The answering machine came on and she heard Grace Appleton's voice.

"Honey, it's Grace. I'm sorry I didn't come today. I know you asked me not to, but I should have come anyway. Please call me if you need anything. I can come down in the morning if you like. Or, you can come up here. Whatever you want. I love you."

Claire let the receiver go into dial tone. Then she walked over and erased the message. She would call Grace later.

Claire took a bottle of wine off the top of the refrigerator and poured herself a liberal serving. Faith, family, and friends all right. And a good dose of this. She smiled.

She went to the living room and turned on the satellite radio to a classical station. Vivaldi's Four Seasons was playing. She liked Vivaldi. She sat in a comfy chair and kicked her shoes off. Sipped the wine and closed her eyes.

The telephone rang again.

She went back to the kitchen, thinking if it was Grace, she would pick up this time because she did not want Grace to worry about her.

But it wasn't Grace. It was Trooper Lytle.

"Mrs. Hannon," — still with that Mrs. shit — "this is Ron Lytle."

Fuck, using his first name now.

"— there's been a break in the investigation. We have a suspect now. I don't want to get your hopes up, but —"

Claire picked up the telephone.

"Hey," she said.

"Oh, hi. You're home."

"Yeah. What have you found out?"

"We received a tip that the murderer is a professional thief named Daniel Bridger. White male, approximately forty years of age. Graying hair, about six foot two. A big man."

"Have you caught him?"

"No. He resides in Baltimore. The Baltimore police have staked out his home and his place of business. But they haven't found him. They will though."

"Do you know where he is?"

"No, Claire. I'm sorry, we don't. But he won't be loose for long. If he hasn't left the country, we'll get him. And I doubt that he's left the country."

"Why?"

"What?"

"Why do you doubt that he's left the country?"

"Well . . . most of these cat burglars, they're just born losers. They don't know how to leave the country. They're strictly short-term thinkers. Smash and grab and then use the profits to buy drugs. You know how it is."

"I don't, actually."

"Oh . . . well. If it would make you feel better, I could come over."

Claire shut her eyes, opened them. "No, thank you though."

"Really, it's no trouble."

How would your wife feel? Claire thought. "Thank you," she said. "I have a friend coming over."

"Oh. Okay. Well, be sure to lock the doors."

Like my husband did? Claire thought. But kept that to herself. "I will," she said. "Bye."

"Bye."

NINETEEN

A convenience store on Route 1 a few miles north of the bridge over the Susquehanna River. A black Mercury appears on the horizon, slows, then turns into the convenience store parking lot. Parks parallel to a minivan with a family inside, pointed the other direction. The minivan drives away and Bridger can see the storefront now as he lifts the nozzle from the pump and puts it in the gas tank.

He had taken the old highway out of Baltimore, through Belair, going north bit by bit, sneaking into Pennsylvania. There were tollbooths and cameras and state workers on the interstate that ran the same direction twenty miles east. It may have been nothing to get too concerned over, but his gut told him he'd be better hidden on Route 1.

His gut . . . trust your gut, they say. A guy he knew in the Navy had once said, "Yeah,

but what if your gut has shit for brains?"
Bridger thought back to a few days and a
thousand years ago. He knew it was never a
good idea to rush the planning on a job.
The planning and the preparation were
probably seven-tenths of it in the first place.
Along with the discipline to know when to
walk away before it gets bad.

Hadn't he always known that? Since he
got out of prison, hadn't he learned? A
woman unbuckles your belt in a storage
room and you forget the basics? Forget to
do the groundwork. Forget to look for traps.
Forget to say no when the job is rushed.
Forget to remember that when it looks too
good to be true, it probably is.

Years ago, before he found his calling, he
used to seek thrills playing cards. They
would play a form of guts called Bloody
Sevens. Draw another seven after staying in
and you lose, automatically. It was one of
those games that was exciting and, with no
pot limit, quickly lucrative. The sort that
triggers the high that comes with gambling
and gets people to make stupid bets. There
was a sailor from Nebraska who enjoyed
looking at the losing hands, shaking his head
and saying, "That was just greed." You
didn't look at the cards, you looked at the
pot and decided to go for it. The mark of

an inexperienced chop.

Maggie had told him about a multimillion-dollar coin collection. Four million dollars' worth and with a twenty percent fence they would split eight hundred thousand dollars. She had told him that and he quit looking at the cards, his eye on the pot . . . and her body. Stupid. Fucking stupid.

Bridger took the nozzle out of the tank and put it back in the pump. He walked into the store to pay for the gas. He handed the woman three twenty-dollar bills and put a couple of banana taffy chews on the counter. She gave him his change and he walked back out to the car.

Got behind the wheel and thought, did she con him?

Had she intentionally lied to him, intentionally put him in this?

It was something he had to think about. He had to think about it whether he wanted to or not. In the life he had chosen, there was a never-ending supply of liars and losers. People lied when they didn't even need to. Maybe it was the same everywhere else, but who could tell. Maggie Chan had been a part of this underground life where people don't fill out tax forms and work nine to five and keep stacks of cash hidden in out of the way places and safety deposit boxes.

After retiring as a prostitute, Maggie Chan had been the wife of an enforcer for the outfit who fucked up and got himself killed. She knew how it worked.

But was she a liar?

He remembered having dinner with her once and she casually told him a story about a trick she'd once had where a guy gave her two thousand dollars to do stuff with his wife while he watched. The point of the story had something to do with the wife having a bizarre name for her vagina or some stupid shit. It was that that made the story interesting to Maggie, not the fact that she took money to perform a lesbian act. At some point Bridger must have made a face of disapproval or even disgust because before he knew it she was getting on to him, a thief, for judging her and thinking she was a low person.

She had said, "I'm not ashamed that I did that. Why should you be?"

"I didn't say I was," Bridger said.

"Yes, you did. It's in your eyes."

"Shit. Look, don't you see? That guy used you. He and his wife both."

"I used them. I got two thousand dollars for it. Who cares?"

"I care."

"God, listen to yourself. What does it have

to do with you? I didn't know you then. It was before Jack."

"Would it have made a difference if you had?"

"Had what?"

"Had known me back then."

"Oh, Christ, Bridger. Listen to what you're doing now."

"What do you mean?"

"Look, you've slept with prostitutes before, right?"

"Yeah, sure."

"I don't judge you for that."

"That's not the point."

"What is the point?"

"I didn't —"

"You didn't what? . . . Marry them? Date them? Make friends with them? You didn't take them to nice restaurants and treat them like ladies?"

"I get your point. I didn't treat them the way I treat you. I didn't get involved with them. I know your past; I've never asked about it. I never asked you to justify it."

"When you give me those looks of disapproval, that's exactly what you're asking me to do. You want me to say some stupid shit like, 'Oh, that was when I was young and I was taking drugs and I was making a lot of bad decisions . . .' You want me to say

146

that so *you* feel better. You want me to apologize for it. But I'm sorry, Dan. I don't owe you that."

"I didn't say you owe me anything."

"What I owe you is the truth. That's it. I'm not going to lie to you about what I am so you feel more comfortable. I'm not gonna do it."

She had been holding her finger up at that last part. She would do that sometimes when she got pissed off about something. He liked that gesture. Missed it now. People would see the two of them together in public, the tall white dude with the little China babe and maybe some of them thought the dude had got himself a nice, little submissive Asian girlfriend. Right.

She had not been a woman to be pushed. She was a mercenary and a hustler. She liked money and she liked sex and for her the two could be connected or not connected, depending on the situation. But she didn't lie. Lying was beneath her.

Bridger drove the Mercury out into traffic. The convenience store faded into the background and he was in country again, the faint smell of tobacco fields coming through the air vents.

So if Maggie had not lied to him, she had to have been convinced by someone else

147

that there was an actual coin collection in that house. She had been conned. Conned by the same people who murdered her. The same people wanting to put him in jail. The same people who wanted Judge Joseph Cannon dead.

The way Bridger saw it, he could go back to Baltimore and ask people Maggie knew who she had seen, but he figured it wouldn't do much good. And even if it did, the Baltimore police were now looking for him. So the only way he had of finding out what was behind this was to check out Hannon. Or people close to Hannon. It would be a way to find out who wanted the man dead. It would be nice to clear it all up and get the police off his back so he wouldn't have to live underground or, worse, go back to prison. But if he couldn't do that, he would settle for killing the people responsible for bringing him and Maggie into it.

He was in Pennsylvania forty minutes later and decided he should bed down for the night. So he stopped at a small town and used cash to pay for a room at a roadside motel. Sat through the second half of a sit-com episode he vaguely recalled seeing before until the Philadelphia news came on.

That was when he learned that the woman who had been in bed with the judge and had died with him was not the judge's wife. The wife — the one who had seen him in the coffee shop — she was still alive.

TWENTY

Trooper Lytle said, "You ever eat here?"

Trooper Pierce said, "No." He didn't say anything else. His wife liked to go to Outback Steakhouse and didn't mind waiting in line to do it. Pierce thought the place was too bright and colorful, but he was one who knew to pick battles and he went along with it.

"Nice place," Lytle said, nodding his head. "Very nice."

Frères-Laval, owned and run by Claire Laval. *It rhymed,* Lytle thought. The father was gone now, why not name it Frères-Claire? Maybe he'd ask her today. Wait until Pierce was gone to do it. He looked at his watch. Quarter till eleven. Shit. Maybe they could stretch the interview and he could take Pierce aside and ask him to help a brother out and beat it after about thirty minutes so he could take the lady to lunch and they could be alone together. Get her by herself and tell her about the time he arrested the notorious Colombian drug lord. Maybe she'd seen it in the newspapers, though it had been four years ago.

She came out of the back office with another nice honey, maybe a few years younger. Talking about something and Claire handed the girl a clipboard and the girl walked off.

Claire walked over and said hello to both of them. She asked them if they wanted to sit at the bar and Lytle said, "Sure."

Early and quiet. The restaurant was not open yet, and soft morning light angled in from the windows. Claire turned to Pierce first and asked him if he would like coffee. Pierce said yes and Claire went behind the bar and brought him a white cup on a matching saucer. She noticed that Pierce held the saucer delicately for a big man.

Pierce took a manila envelope out and put it on the bar. Opened it and slid out a piece of paper they had gotten the night before.

The summary sheet listed the following:

Daniel William Bridger — WM, DOB: 7 Jul 1966, SSN: 447-74-4484. Arrested 15 August 1993 by Indianapolis Police Department on charges of Obstructing/ Resisting Arrest, Armed Robbery, Break-

Then he slid a photograph out. A booking photo, one facing, one turned to the right.

Claire looked at the summary sheet and said, "That's it?"

"What do you mean?" Pierce said.

"That's his entire record?"

"Yeah," Lytle said. "One conviction. But with guys like this, there's probably a dozen things he's done he wasn't charged with. You know, your typical fucking loser."

Claire drew breath and jumped.

"Something wrong?" Lytle said.

"The picture. I've seen him."

"What?" It was Pierce speaking now.

"I've seen him. I saw him."

"Where?"

"At the coffee shop." Her voice broke. She regained it. "I saw him at the coffee shop that very morning. I stood right next to him. Oh, God. I saw him. I — I think I said good morning to him. Or something. I saw him."

Pierce said, "What was he doing there?"

"I don't know. It was in the morning."

Lytle said, "He was probably following her."

"No," Claire said.

"What do you mean, no?"

152

"No. I mean — he was standing in front of me."

"Did he say anything to you?"

"No. I mean, maybe."

"What?" Lytle said.

"I mean, I probably said good morning to him or something —"

Lytle said, "Why would you do that?"

"Do what?"

"Why would you talk to him?"

"I don't know, I just — it's people in a suburban coffee shop."

Pierce said, "And you think it was this man?" Gesturing to the arrest photo.

"Yes. Yes, he's older now. His hair is graying, a little. But that's him."

Lytle said, "What were you doing talking to him?"

"You already asked me that. I wasn't talking to him. I just said good morning. Or, it's going to be a nice day or something. I don't know. Look, that was it."

Trooper Lytle was still looking at her. And Claire didn't know whether to laugh at the man or smack him. Acting like a boyfriend or something.

Pierce was looking at Lytle now, nothing on Pierce's mind but the work. Pierce said to Lytle, "What do you think he was doing there? Rod?"

"What?"

"What do you think Bridger was doing there?"

"I don't know. Following her, I guess."

Pierce turned to Claire. "That's all he said? Good morning?"

"Something like that," Claire said. "Just . . . morning talk. He didn't seem like . . ."

"A killer?" Lytle said. "Sociopaths often don't. They wear a mask, Claire."

Oh, Jesus, Claire thought. The man had cast himself in a TV show. "Well," she said, "he just seemed . . . normal looking."

"He's a thief," Lytle said. "And a murderer."

Claire said, "Is it enough? Do you have enough to put him in jail?"

"I don't know," Pierce said, before the other could give her any more false hope. "We have some evidence. A tip from an anonymous caller. And his description matches that given by the witnesses who saw him run from the police and steal a car. And now we have your statement. But . . . it's not necessarily proof that he killed your husband. We'll have to get ahold of him and question him."

Claire said, "He'll do that? He'll let you question him?"

"We'll see," Pierce said.

Lytle said, "We'll get him, Claire. Now that you've verified that he was here, we can put his photo out to the media. Put it in the newspapers and on television. It's just a matter of time."

And Claire thought, *before what?*

The man handing her a stir stick to put in her coffee cup. Their hands not touching, but holding, for a moment, the same physical object. The same man who probably killed her husband. Right fucking there, close enough to reach out and grab her by the throat.

Had he followed her there? Had he followed her after that? Had he known that she was on her way out of town? Was shooting Joe and his lover nothing more than an action to him? Like getting coffee at a coffee shop? Had it been so easy for him?

She said, "You are going to get him, then? You feel confident of that?"

"We'll get him," Lytle said. "You got my word."

Trooper Pierce was looking at his notes. He did not look up.

TWENTY-ONE

Again the trooper wanted to come back to check on her after she left the restaurant for the night. Claire said no, she would be all right. And Trooper Lytle said he was only concerned for her safety. Claire said she knew that and she knew where to reach him and finally they wrapped up the telephone conversation. Claire remembered that she didn't like the look on the detective's face when she had told him she had met the suspect in the coffee shop. It shouldn't have meant anything, but the detective seemed to want to treat it as something personal between them, rather than a relevant piece of evidence in the investigation. Like he and she should get together and discuss the man and "get past" this issue between them. Maybe say, "Hey, it's Ron here. Is there something else you want to tell me?"

To a degree, it was a cultural difference between them. Claire was the daughter of a

Frenchman and had grown up around what passed for a hoity-toity restaurant. A Main Line girl. Her contact with police officers had been limited. She liked to think that she did not look down on Trooper Lytle because he was a law enforcement officer who wore white oxford shirts from Penneys. She liked to think that, though she wasn't sure that was altogether true. But it wasn't really a matter of class so much as it was . . . *class.* She liked the other detective, Pierce. He seemed like a decent man. A professional. The other one seemed less concerned about her having lost a husband than he was about getting in her pants.

She thought, you could report him. Call . . . whoever it was he answered to and say that he was making her uncomfortable. Why? Had he made a pass at her? Well, no. He just makes me uncomfortable . . . she knew when a man was coming onto her. And they'd say, is that all? Is it possible you're a vain, self-absorbed bitch who's imagining things? Some grieving widow she is; her husband's not dead for two days and she's complaining about some . . . *ruffian* police officer with bad table manners. Vulgar, just simply vulgar. What else, lady? He leave scuff marks on your *grahnd pi-ahno?*

Shit. She didn't have time for this. If she made such a call, then she'd have something else to worry about. An investigation about another investigation. A waitress on her shift once told her a sharp heel on a man's foot topped a sexual harassment complaint any day of the week. Yeah . . . maybe. Meanwhile, the man who killed her husband was out roaming God knows where.

She closed the restaurant at ten o'clock and began the walk out to her car parked behind the restaurant. And she heard it before she saw it, then lights came around the corner, lighting her up, and it was happening so fast, the red windowless van screeching to a halt and the door sliding open before it even stopped and two men in ski masks jumped out, swarming on her, one grabbing her from behind and the other backhanding her across the face, slapping the scream off her, then putting a damp cloth on her face, covering her nose and mouth and she tried not to inhale it but it was no good and by the count of five she was out.

They put her in the van and closed the door, moving out of the parking lot and into the street.

The driver was a guy named Gist. Kenny D

had worked with him before. He was young and mean, younger than Kenny, but he wasn't good at being cool and thinking things out and Kenny had to take off his ski mask so the guy would listen to what he was saying.

"Hey," Kenny said. "*Hey.* Slow down, you fucking idiot. You want us to get pulled over?"

They were in traffic now, not on the highway yet, but it was a long way to the woods in Bucks County.

The driver said, "Sorry, Kenny."

"Don't say you're sorry. Just keep it under the speed limit," he said. "We got about an hour to go. No hurry." Kenny turned to look at the big man in the back of the van with him, whose name was Trent. Kenny smiled and said, "Good-looking piece, huh?"

"Yeah," Trent said.

"Yeah," Kenny said, "well, don't get any ideas. The man said we take her up north, kill her, and bury her. That's all, *capische?*"

The man named Trent didn't respond. He was thinking, *these guys work for the Italians too long, they start talking like them.*

An hour and twenty minutes later, they had parked the van on wet ground in a wooded

159

area. Tall trees and they could hear night sounds. The city dwellers uncomfortable, though not unnerved by the unfamiliar sounds of nature. Thick woods where a body could be hidden and never found.

They took the woman out of the van and set her on the ground about twenty yards away. Then they got shovels out of the van and started to dig a hole. Kenny brought gloves along so Gist and Trent wouldn't get blisters, but he didn't do any digging himself. He just stood next to them, smoking a cigarette like a foreman, a nine-millimeter automatic stuffed in the front of his pants.

Gist said, "Fucking cold out here."

"Yeah," Kenny said, "but the ground is wet. We should be outta here in twenty minutes."

Trent was thinking it was cold too, but he was still looking at the lady lying nearby, looking at the way her white legs stuck out of her black skirt, wondering if he could do it in this temperature and if Kenny D would change his mind. They were out here now with no one around, what difference would it make? He looked at the gun tucked in Kenny's waist, wondered now if the man would be willing to use it over a woman who was going to die anyway . . .

Then saw light on the gun. Light on all of

them now, from a car coming toward them, and stopping as a man stepped out of the car and Kenny didn't wait but raised his arm and fired, the shots shattering the quiet sounds of the woods as the man from the car was firing back and then Kenny and Gist and Trent were moving as Kenny kept firing and they all took cover behind the van.

Trent took a Mac-10 machine gun out of the van and Kenny made a gesture and then Trent was peering around the side of the van, then firing off a burst as the man from the car took off running, back to his car, getting in it and shutting the door and Trent fired off another burst, but kept his finger down on the trigger as the machine gun roared into the night and shattered the windshield. Kept the trigger down until he was sure the guy was either dead or thinking about getting the hell out.

Kenny went around the other side of the van to see if he could sneak around behind the car and take the guy from behind, if he was still alive. Trent was between Kenny and Gist, a pistol in his hand, but not sure whether he should go with Kenny or stay behind the van with Gist . . . he was favoring staying with Gist.

They heard the car engine turn.

And Kenny thought, *Shit, he might get away. Whoever he is.*

But heard the car's engine roar and realized that it was coming toward them.

Trent got behind the van again, resetting the Mac-10 to fire another round, but confused now, disoriented in the dark and the woods and hearing the car get closer, then closer, then punched back on his ass as the car hit the van on the other side.

The car backed up about twenty yards, Trent was getting his bearings, reaching for the machine gun, looking off to his right to see Gist moving away from the van, thinking, *what are you doing?* . . . then hearing the car accelerate again as it came back and slammed into the van again, this time tipping it and Trent screamed as he saw it go past the point of its apex and it came down on top of him and crushed him to death.

Gist managed to get out of its path, his gun at his side, screaming now in fright and looking off to see where Kenny had gone and then he looked back to the van as Bridger came around the side of the van and shot Gist three times and put him down.

Kenny D was in front of the van and standing in the darkness and he heard the shots crack out and saw Gist go down and

knew that the man was dead, Kenny looking at the van lying on its side, knowing
someone was on the other side of it. He
looked behind him, saw nothing but woods,
then looked over to the black Mercury that
had smashed into the van. Then looked back
over to the van.

Slowly, Kenny started stepping toward the
van, raising both his arms, one hand cupped
under the other as he extended his pistol to
fire at the man when he peered around the
corner of the van. Squinting in the dark,
stepping closer, then closer.

"You want to live?"

A voice behind him and he knew before
turning that the man was standing behind
the black Mercury now and Kenny D
flipped around, making a decision in that
instant to go for it, and the shots cracked
out one after the other, but Bridger was
ready and he shot first, putting one in the
man's back and then two more into him as
he went down. Bridger walked over to him.
Bent down and took the gun away from him
before he felt for a pulse. Shit. He was dead.
He wouldn't be able to tell him anything.
Dumb ass. Bridger searched the man's
pockets. He didn't find any identification.
Probably an experienced criminal, though
you could tell that just by looking at him in

the woods with guys with shovels.

Bridger walked over to the woman lying on the ground. Bent down and touched her neck. She was alive. He turned to look back at the Mercury and its smashed-up front. He sighed. Well, with any luck, it would get them to another vehicle.

TWENTY-TWO

The assistant manager of the restaurant noticed Claire's car was still in the parking lot when he came to open the next morning. He presumed that she had come early and opened herself. But then found that Claire was not inside. Phone calls were placed, including Claire's cell number. By the lunch hour, both state and local police were in the restaurant. A missing persons report at that stage, but the cops didn't look too optimistic and a few of the employees of Frères-Laval were crying in the bar area.

In the parking lot of the restaurant, Troopers Pierce and Lytle traded theories. Lytle said maybe she was visiting her friend in New York again, but Pierce said, no, he had already checked on that.

Lytle said, "You think Bridger killed her?"

"Why would he?" Pierce said.

"What?"

"Why would he, I said. He's a thief. Not a killer."

"He's got a record."

"For theft. A cat burglar. Not a killer for hire."

"We have evidence that puts him in the home. That puts him in the area."

"I know, but . . . the woman was in New York at the time. The theory we've been going on is, he broke into the house to rob them, a home invasion, and for some reason or another, killed the people inside."

"He didn't want to leave witnesses."

"But Claire Laval is not a witness. She wasn't there when he broke into the home."

"But she says she saw him. At the coffee shop that morning."

Pierce said, "That bother you?"

Lytle looked at the other detective then to see if there was anything hidden there. Decided there wasn't. He said, "What do you mean?"

Pierce said, "She says she saw the man. What is that about?"

"I don't know — maybe she was meeting him there."

"Meeting him? You mean . . . what do you mean?"

"I don't know, I'm just thinking out loud. Her husband was being unfaithful to her."

"Right . . ."

"And then she disappears."

Pierce remembered the woman telling them that she saw the suspect. And if he hadn't remembered, he had written it down. He was a believer in writing things down. Pierce said, "I don't know, Rod. She doesn't strike me as the type. Besides, she told us she saw him. That's not an indication of guilt."

Lytle said, "Maybe she was covering herself. Maybe someone she knew saw her with the guy at the coffee shop."

". . . I don't know."

"Look, Harold, I'm not accusing her or anything. But we have to think these things out."

Pierce said, "You think she's alive?"

"I kinda doubt it," Lytle said. "Maybe she planned something with this guy. You kill my husband and his mistress, you can take what you want from the house. Or maybe she gave him something else. And then things got out of hand, he almost got caught. Now he's on the run. Wanted for breaking and entering and two counts of murder. And maybe he decided it would be better for him if she disappeared. Before she could tell us anything." Lytle said, "What do you think?"

"I think you're off," Pierce said. His voice firmer than usual. "I'm sorry, but you asked and that's what I think. She told us that she saw the man. And I think she was being truthful. And I don't think she told us that for the purpose of preemption."

"Well, sometimes these nice little ladies from the Main Line aren't as nice as they seem."

"And sometimes they are. In any event, we don't have any evidence to support your theory at this time."

Lytle was about to say, "You mad at me, Harold?" Call the guy out. See if he had taken an interest in the broad. Or take him down a peg for challenging him.

But before he could say anything, Harold had walked off, his writing pad in his hand.

At the FBI office downtown, Adam Roarke looked at the local news on the *Philadelphia Inquirer*'s website, clicked his mouse on the X button and got it off his screen. He walked in shirt-sleeves down to Zabriskie's office and went in and shut the door behind him.

Zabriskie was on the telephone, sounding like he was in a good mood. Looking up, then gesturing to Roarke that he was in the middle of something, Roarke then mouthing and almost whispering, "Get off the damn phone."

Zabriskie sighed, "Listen, I'm sorry. I'm going to have to call you back." He put the phone down. "What, Adam?"

Roarke said, "The woman's disappeared."

"Who?"

"The judge's wife, she's disappeared. We have to tell someone."

"Who are you talking about?"

"*Goddamnit, Sam.* Judge Hannon's wife has disappeared. Blanco is behind it, I know it. We have to do something."

"Slow down, Adam. Sit down."

"No, I'm not sitting down, Sam. I'm going to stand."

"Oh." Zabriskie's tone was one of disappointment. "What are you upset about?"

"Sam, we have to tell people what we know. They think it's some cat burglar that's behind this."

"Yes, for good reason, apparently. People saw Bridger running from the scene."

Son of a bitch, Roarke thought. *So he has been keeping up with it. Son of a bitch.*

Roarke said, "Sam. Presuming that that's the guy that did it, do you really believe that Nick Blanco's not behind it? Two black males killed John. This other guy, Bridger, don't you think he's connected to Blanco as well?"

"First of all, we don't know that the black males are connected to Nick Blanco. So put that out of your mind right now. Second —"

"Sam, these things are related. How can they not be related? They were onto John, they were onto Judge Hannon. And now the man's wife has disappeared. We have to do something."

"Do you know for a fact that she's been abducted? Do you know for a fact that she's been murdered? Do you?"

". . . no. But —"

"And yet in spite of that, you're willing to risk compromising the investigation."

"*What* investigation? We have no investigation left. Our target was Joe Hannon. He's dead now. What investigation?"

"It's an ongoing investigation, Adam."

"What's ongoing?"

"Organized crime. Haven't you figured that out by now?"

Sam's phone buzzed. It was the receptionist. "Sam, Tim is on line two."

Tim Carruthers, the Special Agent in Charge, or SAC. He and Sam were on very good terms. A warmth and bonhomie, of sorts, between them that did not extend to

Adam Roarke. Something Roarke was well aware of.

Sam pointed to the phone. "I have to take this."

It was intended to bring their discussion to an end. It did.

TWENTY-THREE

Claire woke up in a bed with a blanket on top of her.

She blinked and looked up at the ceiling and for a moment she thought she was in her own bed in her home. Or, rather, not her own bed, but the bed in the guest room. The bed in her bedroom that her husband had been murdered in, the mattress and blankets and sheets had all been taken away. Stained with blood and flesh and bone and other bits of evidence. The bedding had not yet been replaced — there hadn't been time — and even if it had, she doubted she would have been able to sleep in that room again. Maybe not ever.

It was a house she had inherited from her family. And now she wasn't even sure she wanted to live in it anymore. She could put it on the market, maybe sell the restaurant too and move someplace else. Maybe until she felt normal again, maybe indefinitely.

She had slept in the guest room since the murder. A smaller room with a smaller bed. But she had not slept well. Since her father's death, she had forgotten how physically exhausting grief could be. Yet she had not been able to get a full night's sleep since the murder.

Until . . . what? Last night?

Last night, she had been abducted.

This was not her bedroom. This was not her guest room.

This was a place she had never seen before.

Claire blinked again.

Her head hurt, and she was aware of a funny, unpleasant smell around her nose and mouth. They had put something on her face. Chloroform. The stuff they used to kill bugs with in her high school biology class. Was that chloroform or something else? Men in masks grabbing her and putting a cloth over her face.

She lifted the blanket off her. Sat up and swung her legs out and put her feet on the floor. She looked down at her feet. No shoes. Where were her shoes? She looked around the room, but did not see them. Where were her shoes?

She checked herself. Her skirt was on. Her underwear was on. Her bra and sweater

173

were on and did not feel like they had been removed and replaced. In short order, she had no reason to believe she had been molested while she was unconscious. None that she could think of anyway, and she didn't want to think about it too much.

She stood and walked over to the closed bedroom door. Stopped and put her ear to it. No sound. No television or radio. No one talking. She tried to peer through the crack in the door, but she couldn't really see anything.

She thought she could open the door and walk out, but the odds were that the people who grabbed her were probably on the other side of it. They would rush her, grab her and then maybe rape her, the sort, maybe, that enjoyed a woman when she was struggling.

The sleep was off her now and she could feel her heart pounding. She had to get out of here. Get away from this place. It was a nice room with clean blankets and sheets, but it was alien to her. It was not a hospital or a cot at a police station. It was a strange house and men wearing ski masks had abducted her. She had to get away from this place. Then think things out.

She turned from her place at the door and looked about the room. Over there, behind her, a window. An old window, one without a screen. The kind that you turn a handle on and the window opens out like a small door. She realized then that she was in an older house.

She walked to the window and looked out of it.

She was on the second floor. Trees out there among a gray morning sky. But there was a roof sloping down to an eave. A roof she could step out on, step carefully until she found a place where she could climb down, maybe even jump off if the ground below was soft enough. She looked down at her bare feet again. Shit.

She turned and looked back at the door. It was still closed. *Why wouldn't it be?* she thought. She put her hand on the handle of the window and applied pressure. It didn't move. She applied more pressure. Nothing. Took her hand off, then put it back on and tried harder. And felt it give. And when it gave, it squeaked.

Christ.

Her shoulders hunched, as if it would somehow dissipate the sound. She turned to look at that door again. Nothing there but the closed door.

She turned back to the window and twisted the handle again. This time, it turned all the way and the window popped open.

She stopped then. Noise coming in from outside now, coming in from the crack. Not city noise. Not traffic or people. But country noise. Nature. Birds chirping, that sort of thing. She smelled clean country air and took notice of the woods again. The air was colder than she thought it would be. Perhaps they were in a cabin. Maybe in the Poconos. She pushed the window open further.

The door opened behind her.

She gasped and turned around. And saw a man step inside the room. Then stop and stand in front of the doorway. The man was tall and broad shouldered and he was holding a gun at his side, the barrel pointing toward the floor. His expression was not angry or even agitated, but almost disappointed. Like a high school principal. She looked at him more, processing him, and then knew that she had seen him before. In a coffee shop near her home. And saw that he remembered her too.

They both stayed where they were, Bridger in the doorway, Claire standing by the open window.

For a few moments, neither of them said anything.

Then Claire said, "You killed my husband." She didn't plan to say it, didn't even really think about saying it. It just came out.

Bridger said, "No, I didn't. Someone else did and set me up to take the fall for it."

Claire felt her heart pounding again. She put her hand on the windowsill to steady herself, wondering if she would be able to be brave before the man raised the gun to kill her.

She said, "I don't believe you. You're just a filthy, cheap murderer. Go ahead and shoot me, you fucking coward."

For a moment, Bridger just looked at the woman. He had not expected her to say what she said. He had expected her to think it, maybe. But he had not imagined she would actually say it. It perplexed him.

He said, "You're not going to get very far without your shoes. And without a coat, you might get sick with exposure."

"Or I might get dead when you shoot me."

"Yeah, that might happen too. Let's go in the kitchen, so you can eat something."

"Or what? You'll use that?"

"Yeah," Bridger said. He gestured for her to move. "Come on."

He walked out of the bedroom behind her. A small room of sorts. A living room, though it was upstairs. Claire wondered if there was a separate unit on the lower floor and, if so, if there was anyone there. There was a fireplace with a fire going.

Bridger pointed to the kitchen area. "There's food in the refrigerator. Coffee in the freezer. Make whatever you like."

"Are you making me cook for you?"

"No. I already ate. If you're not hungry, that's fine. But I imagine you are."

She looked at him. He was across the counter from her now. He looked back at her, then moved around and took a seat at a small table in the kitchen. Put one arm on the table, the gun about six inches from his hand. Apparently he didn't want to hold on to the thing too long.

Claire said, "I am hungry." She wondered if she should have acknowledged it to him. Maybe she should have said nothing to him and just started going to work. The key being not to engage with him. He didn't deserve to be conversed with.

She took a skillet out of the oven and set it on the stove. She took two eggs and some olive oil from the refrigerator. She poured a dollop of oil in the skillet and turned a low flame underneath it. She returned to the refrigerator and checked the date on a carton of milk and saw that it was okay. She broke the eggs into a bowl, using one hand, and poured some milk on top.

Then she opened a drawer to look for a whisk. When the drawer was open, she saw that there was one. Next to a large butcher knife with a black handle.

"You don't want to do that," Bridger said.

Claire looked over to him. He was still at the table and his hand was still off the gun, though it seemed to her that it was closer to his grasp than it had been. *How?* she thought. He could not have seen the knife from there.

Claire said, "Is this your house?"

"No."

"Whose is it?"

It belonged to someone that he had once robbed. Someone he knew from personal experience would not be here during the week. "A friend's," Bridger said. He was not going to say anything else.

She took the whisk out of the drawer and slammed the drawer shut. Using the whisk, she broke the yokes open and began to whip them into the milk.

Bridger said, "Does your head hurt?"

She turned to look at him again. Partly, she expected to see him smiling. But he wasn't.

She said, "Yes, it does."

"There's Tylenol in the cabinet above the refrigerator. Or you can make yourself some coffee. It might help."

She was still looking at him.

"How did you know my head hurt?"

Bridger said, "Because those men held chloroform against your face. It'll do that."

"Those men," she said. "You mean, your men."

"No," he said. "Not my men. I didn't even know them."

"They out getting groceries?"

"No."

"You say you didn't know them. How did you know about the chloroform?"

"I could smell it on you. I washed it off."

"You touched me?" Frightened when she asked the question, but she thought she better ask it before she was too scared to say what was upsetting her.

He held up a hand. "I used a washcloth to clean your face. That's it."

Claire touched her cheek. Maybe it was cleaner than it had been. She said, "Where are the other two?"

"What — the other two guys?"

"Yes. There were three of you. One driving the van, the other two were the ones that grabbed me. You were the one that grabbed me from behind."

Bridger looked directly at her. He said, "You sure about that?"

Claire examined his face. There had been a black ski mask. So what would his face tell now? But she looked at the rest of him. A bigger man than average, but not heavy-set. No stomach. The man who had grabbed her from behind had been wider around the hips and body. The man sitting at the table — the man she had seen at the coffee shop — it was not the same man.

Claire said, "But you must have been there. I don't know why you insist on playing this game with me. You were there. You had to have been."

"I saw it," Bridger said. "Sort of. I was parked outside your restaurant. And I saw the van follow you back to your car, then saw it come back out and your car left behind. So, yes, I put it together. Followed them out to Bucks County."

"Why didn't you call the police?"

Bridger looked at her for a moment. He said, "Followed them out to Bucks County and when I saw them take your body out of the van, I had an idea of what they had in mind."

"And what was that?"

"What do you think, lady? They take you out to the woods in the middle of the night, what do you think they're going to do?"

Claire swallowed it down. The man

181

seemed to be making a point of not telling she was going to be killed and buried. Maybe raped too. Like, she could have the drama of actually hearing the dreadful words, but she was a grown woman and what would be the point.

Claire said, "That's a convenient story. But you still haven't told me where they —"

"They're dead."

"Dead?"

"Yep."

"All three of them?"

"Yes."

". . . did you?"

"Yeah."

She did not look away from him then. The man sitting calmly at a kitchen table, acknowledging that he had killed three men like it was a household task. *Honey? You don't have to set the table, I already took care of it. Oh, and those three guys? I took care of them too.* It should chill her, she thought. Presuming he was not lying about it, it should chill her that a man could be so passive after that. Would he make her feel better by following it up with something like, "Well, it had to be done." Or give her some other tidbit of remorse. Hell, *pretend* for her sake that he felt some. But he wasn't going to do that. There was just . . . what? No maniacal gleam of satisfaction in his expression. No bragging about it. No sign that he had enjoyed it or was ashamed of it. No indication of anything except what he told her.

She asked herself, *What is to stop this remorseless man from sliding his hand to that gun and dispatching her with the same lack of emotion?*

Then he sighed at her and said, "Look, I wouldn't feel concerned about them if I were you. They were going to kill you."

"You mean I shouldn't feel sorry for them?"

"I mean, you shouldn't feel anything. Not remorse, because they don't deserve it. Not fear, because they're not around anymore. Okay?"

Claire said, "That's not what I'm thinking."

"Okay."

"I'm just —"

"You're thinking that I *was* with those guys and that now I'm pretending I'm not."

It took Claire a moment to process it. She said, "Yeah. Kind of."

"Okay," Bridger said. "If I were, and I've got you here now, with a gun and . . . well, why would I lie to you about it?"

"Because you're a sociopath. They lie all the time."

It was a term he'd heard when he was in prison. Sociopath. One without a conscience, likes to manipulate, lives for the short-term kick. Yeah, there were plenty of those in prison. But it was more complicated than that. Or maybe less complicated. The correctional shrinks wanted to be able to categorize them all into things they could name, and stay away from terms like fuck-up, loser, evil, rotten egg, bad seed and/or coldhearted motherfucker. Talking in clinical terms seemed to make things easier for them. It was easier to think that way if you were on the outside. Inside, it was different.

Bridger said, "You own a restaurant, right?"

"Yes."

"Do much psychoanalysis in that line of work?"

"Uh, no. But —"

"So you learned that in college, right?"

"I —"

"Forget it. Listen: I'm not lying to you. Three men kidnapped you. You watch the news, maybe the police will find their bodies. They took you to Bucks County to shoot you and bury you. I got there before they could do it."

"And killed them."

Jesus, Bridger thought. The woman seemed to have her priorities out of order. Out of all this, it seemed important that she be able to judge him for his actions. The old sailors said the American missionaries in China could be like that, right after you saved them from the natives who'd just as soon slit their throats.

"They were going to kill you," he said.

"So you're telling me, you saved my life."

"I'm not telling you that. But, yeah, I did."

"So you could do it later. So you could do it yourself?"

"Uh, no."

"Then why am I here?"

"Because I need you to explain some things to me."

"I don't believe you."

"Lady, I don't care if you believe me or not. I need to find out why those men were after you. To start with."

"Excuse me?"

"I need to find out what you and your husband were into. Because whatever it was, I've been brought into it."

Claire felt disoriented then. It didn't make sense. The things this man was saying, they didn't make sense. Was he for real? Or were these just the sure convictions of a lunatic?

Would he next say, "What's the frequency, Kenneth?" before knocking her to the ground and kicking her senseless? No right answers to his questions because the answers were never the point.

Claire said, "How would I know?"

Bridger said, "You know something. Your husband and his girlfriend were murdered the same night you were out of town. And someone set me up so that I would be there when it happened. Or right after it happened."

Claire opened and closed her mouth. "I had nothing to do with it. I swear."

Bridger stood up and walked over to her. She stepped back when he got close to her. He opened the drawer where she got the whisk and took out the big butcher knife. Looked at her briefly before he stepped back and walked out of the kitchen area, taking the knife with him. "We'll see," he said, and threw the butcher knife on the coffee table in front of the couch.

Then he sat down on the couch, picked up the remote control and turned on the television.

Claire looked over the counter and studied his profile for almost a minute. Then she scooped her scrambled eggs from the skillet into a plate and took her place at the kitchen table.

TWENTY-FOUR

They had taught Kenny not to use his cell phone unless it was absolutely necessary. Cell phone conversation could be picked up on any police car scanner. In fact, there had been a police officer in Darby who got fired after beating up another cop he heard talking dirty to his wife on a cell phone. He'd picked up their naughty talk and giggles and murmurs on a department scanner.

Kenny knew better than that.

So when morning came and Maddox had still not heard from Kenny, he got worried. Kenny would get drunk and get laid and fuck around, but he would do those things after he got to a pay phone and called Maddox and told him it was done. So Maddox could then pass it on to Nick and they could all relax and get back to playing cards or something else worthwhile.

Kenny D was young and he was into the young man's hip-hop sort of thing. He knew

188

names of black guys that did raps and had feuds and he could tell you the difference between East Coast and West Coast rap, statistics of a sort that Maddox had never heard of. Kenny D thought Adam Sandler was funny and his knowledge of Don Rickles was only that he had been in *Casino*. A young man of his time, to be sure. But neither Maddox nor Nick Blanco thought Kenny D was a fuck-up. He would have called by now and let them know it was done. They should've received that call by no later than two A.M.

But they hadn't and that's why Claude Maddox was in his Dodge Charger by seven-thirty that morning and driving up to Bucks County to the place where they had buried another body. If something had gone wrong, it would be better to find out sooner than later.

It occurred to Maddox during the drive that he had never been to this place during the day. Not that he could remember, anyway. The last time he had been there was when they killed the guy who was late on his vig and threw a half-eaten sandwich in Claude Maddox's face. Maddox shot the guy two seconds after that. An unexpected corpse and they had to put him in the trunk of a Ford and run him out of town.

189

Maddox had had mixed feelings about that one. He had killed that man in anger. In hindsight, it was probably a reasonable whack. The guy had dissed him and if word got out, Maddox's reputation would have suffered. But he still wondered if it had been rash. Wondered if it had been lacking a certain amount of style. In any event, it wasn't one that he took any particular pride in.

There had been a job a few years ago that he had taken pride in. It was a job that had moved him up in the Family as well. What had started that one was three guys sticking up a card game in West Chester with a couple of outfit officials. Three guys wearing masks and holding shotguns had scored about forty thousand dollars. Cal Sabatini, a made guy, had been one of the players, along with a couple of civilians. It embarrassed Cal and he gave Nick Blanco the word the very next day that he wanted those three guys found and put down and he wanted it done in the next two days.

Nick gave the job to Claude Maddox.

Okay, yeah . . . detective work. Claude got to drive around the greater Philadelphia area, playing Jim Rockford and asking a lot of questions and deploying other forms of persuasion. By the second day, he found one of the guys and kept him alive until the guy took him to his two buddies. Maddox said something like, "I'm glad we got all this straightened out," before killing all three of them with a forty-five. Blanco gave him high marks for that one.

The Charger passed an Esso station. Claude looked at the odometer and added three miles to the number on the dash. When it got there, he looked out for the dirt road on his right.

Took that through damp, unpaved roads, little bits of gravel pinging against the car, the tall trees shading over it. Veered left at the second turn, kept on that for a couple of hundred yards until it brought him to the clearing that he was familiar with.

Then said aloud, "Jesus Christ."

The underside of the upended van in his sights. And Maddox thought, *it's going to get worse.*

It did.

Blanco said, "When does it warm up?"

"I don't know," D'Andrea said. "I'm ready for it, though."

They were sitting on the bleacher seats again at the New Jersey high school. On the field were a group of girls practicing field hockey. It seemed to put D'Andrea in a bad mood; he would have preferred to watch baseball.

D'Andrea said, "So that's what you call an accident, huh?"

"Hey," Nick said, "it was what they call a random act of violence."

"Getting shot by a coupla niggers? That's an accident."

"Yeah, it is. You complaining?"

A girl with a blonde ponytail whacked the ball past a defender, then took off like a shot, a determined look on her face.

D'Andrea said, "No one's complaining. Yet."

"Ah, shit, Henry. It's done. The black guys are dead and there ain't anything that's gonna come back on us."

"Hmmm," D'Andrea said.

And Nick Blanco thought, *this fuck never gives up.* No pleasing him, so why even bother? He was probably pissed because it *had* been cleaned up. Guys like Henry couldn't handle being content. *Well, fuck him.*

D'Andrea said, "There was nothing in the papers about it."

"About what? The shooting at the bodega?"

"Well, yeah, there was that. But there was nothing about him being a fed."

192

"So what?"

Nick said, "Would it make you feel better if there was?"

D'Andrea shrugged.

Nick Blanco felt better. The man had nothing to add. He just didn't want to give Nick the satisfaction of knowing it was finished. If there were other issues, D'Andrea would be glad to give him shit over them. But there weren't any. Only shrugs and gestures. Nick thought, *He doesn't know.* He doesn't know about Joe Hannon and how bad it could have been. Sitting there in his hat and his camel hair coat, sure of his place in the world, he doesn't know shit. All he's got is body language.

Nick said, "Was there anything else?"

He was pushing it now. Pushing the bigshot from New York. But it was worth it.

D'Andrea gave him a look, and Blanco looked back at him calmly, like he could sit there all morning if he needed to.

"No," D'Andrea said. "Just be more careful in the future."

Nick Blanco smiled. "Sure, Henry. Have a nice drive back."

That was worth it too, Nick thought.

TWENTY-FIVE

"May I ask what your intentions are?"

The woman was standing behind the counter now. She had just put her dish in the sink.

Bridger took his eye off the television screen and put it on her.

"Not now," he said. "Come in here and sit down."

She walked out from behind the counter. She saw he was still holding the gun. He gestured to the chair that sat at a right angle to the sofa. Claire thought, *At least he's not asking me to sit on the sofa with him.*

She said, "I haven't cleaned up."

"Excuse me?"

"I feel . . . I haven't been to the washroom this morning. I need to brush my teeth, wash my face."

"All right."

Bridger stood up and led her to the bathroom. At the door he said, "You can close the door, but I'm going to stand here. If you try to climb out that window, I'll hear it. So don't try, all right?"

He said "all right" in the same tone fathers used on children, Claire thought. Half-order, half-plea. It almost made her smile.

Claire said, "You're the one with the gun."

"Yeah, right." Bridger gestured her in and pulled the door shut afterward. He said to the closed door, "Don't lock it. It's a thin door and I can kick it in."

She locked it anyway.

And said, "I'm not going try to go out the window. You hear me try, kick away."

Shit, Bridger thought. For all she knew, he'd be the sort that would open the door while she was sitting on the toilet, try to get a glimpse of her with her skirt bunched up around her waist. Well, he'd let her have that one. For the first time in days, he smiled. Sort of. She was a little like Maggie, in her way. *You're the one with the gun.*

A few minutes later, Claire was standing in front of the bathroom sink, looking at her reflection in the mirror. Her makeup from the day before was still on and she didn't like the way she looked. She turned on the faucets and used bar soap to wash her face. Rinsed off the soap and the stuff underneath and took another look at herself.

A woman in dire straits. Like someone in one of her mother's Mary Higgins Clark books. A woman in peril. Waiting for the big, strong policeman to come rescue her. Waiting for . . . who? Trooper Lytle?

She wondered about Lytle now. From the time she had met him, he had given her the creeps. A policeman with a badge and a gun, sent to protect her, right? She wondered what it would be like to be alone in a cabin with him. *Christ.* He would be the sort that comes to her room in the middle of the night, a hard-on in his pajamas. She'd have to put a chair against the door before she'd be able to even sleep in the same house with him.

And . . . what? She felt better with this other man? What was it about him that she thought he would not peek through a keyhole to see her use the toilet?

She looked at the door.

Well, to start with, there was no keyhole in the door. So he wouldn't be able to even if he wanted to.

But that wasn't the point. If not, then what was the point? That a woman knows when a man is the sort that rapes and abuses women? Not every woman does know. She thought she knew her husband. But he had been sleeping with another

196

woman. And she hadn't known about that.

She thought, *the man has a gun. He's keeping me here at gunpoint. He's not allowing me to leave. He's kidnapped me. Maybe he doesn't have rape on his mind. Maybe he seemed like a nice guy when he handed me a stir stick at the coffee shop, but for Christ's sake, Claire, don't presume he's somehow safer than a police officer just because he feels somehow . . . less creepy.* That was the sort of mentality that led women to marry imprisoned serial killers through the mail.

She looked at herself in the mirror. No makeup now, her hair a little wet from the rinse and pushed back from her face. She didn't look too bad. She looked okay, in fact. Considering.

She realized her heart wasn't pounding with fear anymore. She thought, *Well, it can't keep doing that forever, can it?* What had she learned in college Psych 101? Something about the worst part about jumping out of an airplane was the wait before the jump.

That was the same course where she had learned the definition of a sociopath. The word she had thrown at the man outside the door. Which seemed to amuse him. Or bore him. Maybe he knew that she hadn't used the word in years. That she didn't know what she was talking about.

She opened a drawer and found a tube of toothpaste and what she hoped was a woman's toothbrush. It looked clean and that was as much thought as she was going to give it. She started to brush her teeth, the cold water running as she did so.

Bizarre, she thought. Brushing your teeth while a man with a gun stands outside the bathroom door. Just . . . nuts. But her hand was steady as she brushed and she felt a little bit of pride as she did it. Proud of herself that she was not falling apart. She held it together even as a thought crept into her mind that she couldn't quite will away. A voice saying, *Proud? Proud of what? If you're not terrified right now, you must be insane.*

Well, maybe so. But if it got her through this, she would accept a little eccentricity in her psyche.

Twenty-Six

Maddox parked the Charger and crossed the street, walking through traffic then getting to the sidewalk and into the diner.

It was a gray, dingy diner where every section smoked and it had stools in front of a counter and booths with brown vinyl seats. Two men of middle years sat on the stools, spaced from each other, and a young, skinny couple were in one of the booths.

Maddox went behind the counter and through the swinging door into the kitchen. The cooks and the guy washing dishes gave him quick glances before going back to work.

Maddox hit the stairwell at the back of the kitchen, climbed stairs and turned the corner on a landing where a large black man was keeping guard. The black guy nodded at Maddox and rapped the door four times, using quick four/four time. The door was unlocked and opened.

A large room with eight green felt tables. The long kind. At each table, a female dealer. Poker, a minimum of seven players at each table. Old guys with track suits and big glasses, a handful of old, rough-looking women sprinkled among them. Younger players wearing sport coats and small-framed sunglasses. Two uniformed cocktail waitresses brought them free drinks when they wanted.

There was no cash on the tables. Chips only. There was a half-hour time period, early in the day, when you could buy in. No exceptions.

Cigarette smoke forming a small cloud amidst murmurs of gamblers and the chinking of poker chips.

Maddox walked through the tables to the closed door of an office on the other side. He knocked on the door.

"Yeah?"

"It's Claude."

"Come on in."

Nick was sitting behind his desk. To his right, there was a half-dressed girl on a calendar, holding some sort of pipe in her hands like it was a dildo. A gift from a guy who owned a natural gas company.

Maddox said, "I just got back from Bucks County. Kenny's dead."

"What?"

"Kenny D is dead. Shot. The guys with him, they're dead too."

"They shoot each other?"

"No. Doesn't look like that. Two guys shot to death, one of them Kenny D. The other guy had a van pushed on top of him."

Nick said, "How?"

"I don't know. Looks like it got hit by a car. Or a bulldozer. I don't know, Nick."

Nick Blanco put his face in his hands for a moment. Pulled them off and said, "The woman?"

"She's not there."

"You sure?"

"Yeah, I'm sure."

"Did you check?"

"Nick, she's not there. I saw the place where they were going to bury her. They'd starting digging. She's not there."

"I don't understand. How?"

"How?" Maddox said. "Well, let's see. She could have got the jump on them. Taken one off in the woods, promising to give him something. Then taken his gun and killed him. Then went back and killed the other two. Like Buffy the fucking vampire slayer. But, that wouldn't explain the van."

"The van . . . ?"

"The van being on its side. Crushing

Trent to death. That was done by somebody driving a car."

"So someone else was there."

"Had to be."

For a moment, neither one of them said anything.

Then Nick said, "I don't like what you're thinking, Claude. If you're thinking it."

"I don't like it either. But it would explain some things."

"You're talking about Bridger, right? You think he was there?"

"Yeah, I do."

"How do you know it wasn't a cop?"

"Would a cop kill three guys and just leave them there? Wouldn't we have seen something about it on the news? The only one that's been out there since it happened is me."

"But how? How could he know?"

"Well, he knows he's been set up."

"But he had no way of tying it to us. Or Kenny."

"Maybe Kenny talked too much. Maybe he was following Kenny."

"Yeah, maybe," Nick said. "Or maybe he was following the woman."

"Why do you think that?"

"I don't know. Shit. We have to find her. See if he's with her."

"If so, maybe he's killed her by now."

Nick said, "That's not really his thing."

"You talking about Bridger now?"

"Yeah."

Maddox had not been told everything. It was Nick's way not to tell everything he was thinking, to give part of a plan to one guy and another part to another guy. It was a style of management that seemed to work for him. Maddox said, "I don't really know this guy. Do you?"

"I know who he is. I don't know him that well."

Maybe that's the problem, Maddox thought. But he didn't say it. He said, "Well, I think maybe it changes things."

"How's that?" Nick said.

"Maybe we can't afford to wait for him to be caught and arrested. Maybe he needs to die too."

"Yeah," Nick said. "He probably does."

TWENTY-SEVEN

He pointed her to the chair and told her to sit down. She did and he took a place on the sofa a few feet away.

Claire asked, "Do I get to wear my shoes?"

"Later," Bridger said. "First of all, did you know those men?"

"The ones that kidnapped me?"

"Yeah."

"No. Only you."

"I told you, I'm not one of them. They're gone now."

The woman didn't respond.

Bridger asked, "You think I killed your husband?"

"The police think so."

"What do you think?"

She seemed to study him for a moment. "I don't know," she said.

Bridger said, "Consider the fact that you're alive now."

"Maybe you've got something else in mind."

Bridger looked at the woman. She was making him think of Maggie again. Talking about it in a way that was direct, but not vulgar. He said, "I don't."

Claire believed him. But she did not want to concede it to him. Not to someone like this. She said, "You've abducted me."

Bridger said, "Consider what I just said and ask yourself, if he didn't kill my husband, who would want to?"

"You mean, if not you?"

"If not me."

She seemed to think this over for a while. Then she said, "I don't know."

Bridger was looking at her, his expression calm. The woman without shoes looking awful cool. He said, "What about you?"

"Excuse me?"

"I said, what about you?"

"Me?"

"Yeah, you. Your husband had a girlfriend. How did you feel about that?"

"That's none of your business."

"It is my business. If you had something to do with his murder, you had something to do with setting me up."

"I don't even know you."

"You could have hired it done. People who

commit crimes would know how to get me there."

"Set up? You say that like you were someone just walking down the street. What were you doing there, anyway? You sit there, indignant, because you might go to prison. But you broke into our home."

"Well . . . that's what I do. I'm a thief. But I don't kill people."

"You're a criminal. It's all the same."

"I don't kill people. And I don't work with people who do."

"A man of principle, huh?"

"No. That's just not my thing. If you know what you're doing, you don't kill or harm anyone."

"You're taking things that don't belong to you. That's harmful."

"Right," Bridger said. He wasn't going to argue with her.

"And you just told me you killed three people."

Bridger sighed. Like, *come on.* "That was different. Listen, did the police tell you about me?"

"Yes. They told me what they knew about you."

"Showed you a picture?"

"Yes. A dated one."

"Did they show you any record of me killing or harming any homeowner?"

"No, they did not. But that doesn't mean anything. I'm looking at you now and you're holding a gun to keep me in this chair."

Jesus, Bridger thought. Like arguing with an assistant D.A. "Listen," he said, "I was in your house because someone had told me there was a coin collection."

"A coin collection?"

"Yeah."

"In our house?"

"Yeah."

"But there isn't."

"I know that."

"Then why did you —"

"I know that *now.*" Bridger said, "Someone told me you had a four-million-dollar coin collection. They told me that to get me to break into your home. They told me that so that I would be in the house when your husband was killed. I was conned. Bad."

Claire seemed to study him. Her first instinct was to say, "That's not my problem."

But then she thought, *it is.* Men in masks had abducted her, and she was beginning to believe this man had not been one of them.

But what if he was lying? Didn't all sociopaths lie? Weren't they all really good at it?

But if he were lying, why would she be

207

alive now? What would he be getting out of this?

Claire said, "You think I had something to do with it?"

"I don't know. I'm trying to find out. Did you?"

"Why don't you just torture me until I tell you what you want to hear?"

Bridger said, "Why don't you cut the melodrama and just tell me the truth? That's all I want."

Claire Laval regarded the stranger for a few moments. It was unreal, still. But somehow more real than what had gone before. A stranger before her.

She said, "The truth is, I didn't even know he was having an affair. And it makes me feel stupid." She was talking quickly now, without thinking about what she was saying. Talking like she hadn't talked since the police had called her in New York and told her her husband was dead. Talking to a criminal because he was here and she needed to talk to someone. She said, "You know? It makes me feel stupid. Do you know how that feels? To feel so — fucking dumb while you're grieving?"

Bridger didn't say anything.

Claire said, "I'm not sure I knew him that well at all. They say a woman always knows, but I . . ." Her voice broke. She regained composure and said, "Sorry."

"It's all right," Bridger said.

It was a quick exchange, over before either one of them knew it. But when the moment passed, Claire's choked-off sob almost turned into a laugh. It was absurd, really. This professional thief offering her compassion now.

Claire said, "Isn't there a name for this?"

"What?"

"The Stockholm syndrome?"

Bridger said, "What's that?"

"Never mind," Claire said. "You still think I had my husband killed?"

"I don't know."

"I don't know about you either," Claire said. She looked at him without looking at the gun. "I really don't," she said, almost to herself.

There was eye contact between them. Brief, then gone.

Bridger said, "Your husband."

"Yes?"

"Did he have enemies?"

"Joe? God. I mean, he was a judge. But . . ."

"A criminal judge?"

"Sometimes. He had a civil docket though, too. But . . . Joe was a politician. He got

209

along with everyone."

"Everyone?"

Claire looked at Bridger. "We didn't fight, Mr. Bridger. We were estranged. They're two different things."

Bridger made a gesture. "Sorry," he said. "What about him? Was he agitated? Nervous or scared?"

"What do you mean?"

"Did he act like he was in trouble?"

Claire was thinking again. His behavior at the restaurant the night before . . . the night before, it had been unusual. Something had been bothering him. Maybe even scaring him.

"Maybe," Claire said.

"What? What was it?"

"He said something about a man getting shot. Like that day."

"Who?"

"What?"

"Who got shot?"

"I don't know. He said it was someone he knew. In South Philly. No. He said he didn't know him. He'd only met him."

"Did you believe that?"

Claire looked up.

"What?" she said.

"Did you believe that?"

She hesitated. It didn't seem right.

"Are you asking if I — if I thought my husband was lying to me?"

"Yes."

"I don't think you —"

"Do you think he knew the guy? Do you think he knew the guy who was killed?"

Claire's expression tightened. "Yes. Yes, I think he did."

"And this scared him?"

"Yes. I think it did."

"Good," Bridger said.

"Good?" Claire said. "You think that's good?"

"Yeah. It helps me."

"Oh, well, good for you."

"Excuse me?"

"Never mind."

"Did he hide things from you?"

Claire was shaking her head. She said, "You shouldn't be doing this. You . . . shouldn't be asking me these things."

"Did he?"

"Yes. I mean, he concealed his emotions from everyone. His fear, his anger. He was . . . good at that."

"That's not what I meant," Bridger said. "I meant, criminal things. Like drugs or a gambling problem."

"I don't know. I don't."

"But you agree that it's possible. Possible

that he was involved in something bad? Maybe in trouble?" He was asking now.

"Yes," she said at length. "It's possible." She looked at the inquisitor. "What difference does it make now?"

"It makes a difference for both of us. Last night, men tried to kill you."

"You say."

"I saw it," Bridger said, and that was good enough for him. "You're ready to accept it, roll over and die, that's your problem. But I'm not ready. And I don't want to go back to prison. Not even for a little while, let alone a lifetime. That's why I'm going to find out who did this."

"The police are already doing that."

"The police have already decided I did it. I know I didn't."

"Say you didn't. Say I'm dumb enough or crazy enough to believe you. What are you going to do if you find the people who did?"

Bridger said, "Have a conversation with them."

"With that?" Claire gestured to the pistol.

"Yeah."

"I lost a husband," Claire said. "You don't hear me talking about killing people."

Bridger shrugged. He still didn't want to argue ethics with her. But the woman was looking at him now with a steady gaze. The same woman he had talked to this morning in the kitchen, the same woman he had taken shoes from. Yet not the same.

Claire said, "Can I ask you something?"

"What?"

"Isn't there someone else you should be questioning?"

"Like who?"

"The man who told you there was a four-million-dollar coin collection in my house."

There was a silence between them, and the change in Bridger's facial expression did not go unnoticed by Claire.

"It wasn't a man," Bridger said. "It was a woman. She's dead now."

". . . did you?"

"No. They did. She was a friend of mine."

After a moment, Claire said, "I'm sorry."

"Yeah, I am too."

They were quiet again. The light outside was softening, the evening coming upon them. Claire was not thinking about escaping now, maybe not even that frightened. A stranger before her. A dangerous man with a gun. Yet at that moment she could not persuade herself that he would harm her. Not right now. She wondered if she was a fool. Someone had said that sociopaths were good at being sentimental. *You remind me of my father, detective. You have a nice way about you, ma'am. My mother didn't love me.* Thinking now not so much of her Psych 101 class, but the Flannery O'Connor short story she had read in high school. The not-so-subtly named "Misfit" struggling with the existence of Jesus before he shot the stupid old woman to death.

Claire squinted. Looked at the man, then looked away.

Was he playing her?

He had not asked for any sympathy. He had not made any excuses. He did not seem the sort who would do that. Like it was beneath him. An integrity of sorts.

Then thought, *integrity? Claire Laval, you are losing it.*

"I'm tired," Claire said. "I'd like to rest for a moment. Do you mind if we stop? For now, that is."

"No, I don't mind." Bridger stood. "You can go in the bedroom, if you like."

"I don't want to go in the bedroom."

Bridger frowned. He didn't understand.

"If I go in the bedroom," Claire said, "I'll feel like I'm being imprisoned there. And I'm tired of feeling like that." She indicated the couch. "Will you switch places with me?"

"You want to lie down here?"

"Yes."

She thought about asking him not to look at her in gross ways or touch her while she slept, but dismissed the thought. The man was no rapist, she believed. That, she was pretty sure of. And she was tired and didn't want to think right now.

"All right," Bridger said.

The woman lay on the couch, looked up at the ceiling then closed her eyes and put her arm over her face. Bridger did look at her, briefly, but only to see that she was not up to anything. When she was asleep, he turned and looked at the blank television screen. He could turn it on, but the sound could awaken her. So he left it off, and looked out the window.

Twenty-Eight

Roarke drove to his athletic club after he left the office. He changed into workout clothes and ran three miles around the track. The oval of the track had a circumference of one-seventh of a mile. He counted his laps and checked the clock every few minutes to see how he was pacing. He tried to concentrate on the running, hoping that it would free his mind up from the events of the day. But it wasn't working. What he kept returning to was not the office, but a memory of his father.

Lee Roarke. There had been a man. A sergeant in the Army. And not just a sergeant, but a drill sergeant. Service in Korea where he took a shot in the lung. The bullet and a good part of the lung removed thereafter. The old man had returned to his cigarette habit after recuperating; two packs a day, Camel filters, and the man seemed to brag about it. He still ran his men on five-mile drills and he was always out front and if he felt any exertion, he never showed it.

One day, when Adam was around ten, he was with his father in Manhattan when they came upon some dopehead smashing in a car window. Lee didn't hesitate. "Stay here," he said and ran up to the dopehead, grabbed him and threw him up against the car. The dopehead, who was himself black, had trouble processing it. A brother in civilian clothes, fucking him up for trying to boost a car stereo. He was dirty and he smelled of urine and Lee eventually released his grasp and the guy ran off.

"Damn," Lee said, because now the car's window was busted wide open and it was just a matter of time before the doper returned or some other bum came along and climbed into the car. So young Adam stayed with his father until the old man flagged a passing police car for assistance.

Two officers, both of them white, looking at the man, but not listening to him as he explained what happened. And Adam saw them arrest his father and take him away.

Later that day, he was released. A patrol commander and a judge apologizing to him, saying this should have never happened.

Adam remembered his parents arguing that night. His mother telling his father he should sue them and get some money out of it. Lee saying, they said they were sorry.

The old man died before Adam graduated from the FBI Academy, though he had been at his college graduation ceremony.

Adam Roarke was thinking about it now. Thinking, *how?* How did he put aside the humiliation of that day? The anger? How did he just put it aside? A man serves his country, fights in a war, gets shot, smokes cigarettes and runs five miles without breaking a sweat. Then, because all that's somehow not enough, he stops the commission of a crime, stays with an automobile belonging to a person he doesn't even know to protect it, and gets arrested for being black. All of that time, all of that effort, wasted.

Wasn't it?

How does a man not break down over that?

Was it a matter of Christian faith? The old man had not even attended church. Would sit in the car, smoking a cigar and reading the paper, while Adam and his sister and his mother were inside. He had never acknowledged any belief in a higher power. Unless you counted the Army.

It was as if showing any weakness, any emotion, was somehow beneath him. For Lee Roarke, there was no talk of the "struggle of the negro." And he was known to give a soldier's weary frown when anyone said anything about working for "the man." The expression not saying, *what can you do,* but rather, *you don't know what you're talking about, punk.*

Adam Roarke himself had been on the receiving end of that expression. Mostly when he was in college and would come home and tell the old man of things he thought the old man did not understand. And it would be years before Adam understood that he was one of thousands of young college students who thought he had it all figured out by the age of twenty-one, but actually knew very little.

Adam sprinted on the last lap, passing people on the left and cutting back in afterward, like he was driving on an interstate. Ran another half-lap full out after that.

When he walked into the locker room, the sweat was pouring off him. And he thought, *I don't even smoke.*

Walking out of the club, showered and back in his FBI clothes, he allowed himself to continue the line of thought. Allowed it even though he was afraid it would make him feel weak and ashamed.

His annual performance evaluations were

coming up. That Sam Zabriskie would have a role in making that evaluation, there was no doubt. He could be an exemplary young agent or a troublemaking nigger.

Adam Roarke thought, *I don't know what to do.*

What would the old man say?

He who had put his faith in the U.S. Army. He had swallowed indignities. Or ignored them. What would the old man do?

Adam Roarke got into his BMW 530i and started it. He liked the car. His wife liked the car too. They had bought it together at a dealership in Long Island. She had been so happy that day. Now, she was clerking for a judge in Manhattan and had a good chance of getting in with a blue chip law firm when it was done. Also in New York.

His wife had said to him once, "We're really very lucky, Adam." He had never figured out what she meant by that. Lucky in spite of being black? Lucky to have good careers? What?

Like a lot of young married couples, they had a plan. Their plan was that Adam would eventually get transferred back to the Manhattan FBI field agency. A home in Long Island. A nice home. Then, within a year or two, start a family. *It was not a lot to ask for,* Adam thought. He had never sought a huge salary. Never sought fame or fortune. He had kept his goals modest.

But young agents with bad evals don't get to pick where they get assigned. No, they don't. If you step on the wrong toes, you get sent out to Omaha or Tulsa. Tell that to the wife and ask how lucky she feels then.

Driving back to his apartment, Roarke thought, *it should not be this complicated.* He had done the right things. He had married the right girl. He had studied and worked hard. He had resisted temptations that would have given him quick gratification. Was it right that it should be this complicated?

And then he realized that he was actually angry at his father. That he actually thought that his father had it better than he had. Because for the old man, it could not have been this complicated.

And he could almost hear the old man saying what he had often said. "Son, you're not making much sense."

A ball game on the television, the Brewers playing the White Sox in the freezing cold of Wisconsin, no sound because he has pressed the mute button. On the coffee table in front of him was his dinner, half-eaten.

She answered the phone on the fourth ring. One more and he would have gotten the answering machine.

"Adam?"

His wife has seen his number on the identifying screen.

"Hey," he said.

"How are you?"

"Oh . . . tired."

"Been busy, huh?"

"Yeah. How was your day?"

"Real busy. We have that class action trial starting tomorrow. It may take three weeks. You know David Boies?"

"No."

"You don't? He's the one that brought down Bill Gates in that antitrust suit."

"Oh, yeah. I've read about him."

"He's representing the class. Brilliant man. Nice, too. He was asking where I was going to work when I finished the clerkship."

"Oh?"

"Well . . . he wasn't offering anything. I think he was just being nice. But, man. It was neat talking to him."

"Well, you never know. You're very good at what you do."

"You're such a nice husband. I haven't even really practiced law yet."

"Well, I have great expectations."

He heard her smile. She liked it when he said things like that. He heard her say, "I do too. Will you be up here Friday night?"

"I think so . . ."

"Great. I love you." She was closing the conversation. He didn't blame her; it was getting late and she had no doubt been working very hard. She had a lot on her mind, and what could he tell her anyway? And he didn't want to think too much about what she meant when she said she had great expectations too. At least not right now. He had started it, after all.

"I love you too," Adam said. "I'll see you soon."

TWENTY-NINE

She lifted her arm off her brow, looked up at the ceiling and blinked. Darker now, faint light coming from somewhere. She looked over and saw Bridger sitting in a chair, a lamp on. He looked back at her, did not smile.

Claire said, "What time is it?"

"Around eight," Bridger said.

"Eight? I slept that long?"

"Yeah."

She sat up. Winced. A pain in her back. She put her feet on the floor. She looked at Bridger and said, "You picked me up in Bucks County and brought me here, right?"

"Right."

"How did you bring me here?"

"In a car."

"You mean, in the trunk of a car?"

"Yeah."

"Jesus."

"Sorry. I couldn't risk having you seen."

"What if I'd suffocated?"

"You gotta be in there a long time for that."

She looked at him again. Well, he'd said he was sorry. She looked at him and then around him.

Claire said, "Where's your gun?"

"I put it away." He did not elaborate.

"I'm flattered," Claire said.

Bridger said, "I made some coffee. Would you like some?"

". . . yes," she said. Feeling strange now, the notion of this man serving her.

"Anything in it?"

Very strange.

"A little milk, if there's any left."

"There is."

He was walking toward the kitchen now, getting a cup out and pouring milk in first so he would not have to stir it. Claire watched him as he did it. *The way his hands move is interesting,* she thought. Almost delicate, particularly for a big man. Like he could have been a chef.

He brought the coffee back and handed it to her.

"Thank you," Claire said, without thinking.

He did not say she was welcome. He just walked back to his chair.

Claire said, "I wanted to ask you something."

"Okay," Bridger said.

"The girl. What was her name?"

"The girl's name?"

"Yes."

"It was Maggie."

"Was she your . . . girlfriend?"

"No, not really. She was a friend. She used to be married to a guy in the outfit."

"Outfit . . . you mean, organized crime."

"Yeah."

"So she was a criminal?"

"Well . . . maybe. She'd been around. Maybe she thought she was. But she didn't really know what she was doing."

Claire said, "I don't understand."

"She came to me and told me about a coin collection. That we could both make a lot of money — I told you this already."

"— yes."

"But, she said it like she believed it."

"Maybe that's what she wanted you to think."

"Maybe. But she's not that great a liar. I think someone persuaded her that it was there."

"Someone from the . . . outfit?"

"Maybe."

Claire said, "You believe that, don't you?

You believe she didn't lie to you."

"Yes."

"You're that sure about her?"

"I'm never that sure of anybody. But . . . it's the thing that makes the most sense."

"You don't think, maybe, that she betrayed you?"

"Betrayed me?" It sounded strange to him. "Lady, in this life you've got pretty much no one you can trust. We don't . . . think in terms of honor or code. But, no, I don't think Maggie intentionally misled me."

"Well, you seem to be going out of your way to cover for her."

Bridger smiled. "Why would I do that?" he said.

"Maybe you were in love with her. Maybe it's too painful to admit that she brought you into this."

"She *did* bring me into this. I'm not struggling with that, if that's what you're thinking. And, no, I was not in love with her. She was a good friend."

"You're not angry at her."

"She's dead now; what would be the point?"

"Well . . ."

"Look, she fucked up. Some piece a shit approached her and told her about a coin collection and she was tempted by the thought of an easy take. Then she came to me and talked me into it. When someone gets taken, they play a role too."

"You mean, because of their own greed?"

"Yeah. Or because they want a kick. Christ, I don't know. We both got taken. And she got killed."

"You think she deserved that?"

"Deserved what? To be murdered? . . . No, I don't think that at all. Christ, I just told you she was a good friend."

"Don't get mad."

"Well, what sort of man do you think I am? You think because I say she fucked up that I believe she deserved to be strangled?"

And now Bridger was picturing it. Maggie lying on the floor of her apartment, the line around her neck left by the garrote. Unmerciful and undignified. Who deserves that?

"No," Claire said. "I didn't mean that." She was watching him. He was upset now, the first time she'd seen him like this. Yet he was not making her afraid. "I'm sorry," Claire said.

He sighed and looked back at her and his expression changed. "It's all right," Bridger said. "I don't know why I'm barking at you. You didn't do anything wrong."

Claire leaned forward. "So . . . you don't

suspect me anymore?"

"No."

Claire was thinking about it now, thinking about how she should phrase it. Knowing that it was best, sometimes, to keep your thoughts to yourself. In business and sometimes in marriage. Thinking, but trusting her gut as well. She knew it didn't make sense. She knew that what they called the Stockholm syndrome could mess with your mind and get you to say and think things that were not rational. She knew all that. But who could explain what had gone on in the last few days? She could not draw on her past for support because her past no longer seemed that solid to her. The past was not a reality, but a perception she had created. And it was past. Now, she was where she was and she had to deal with things as they were.

Claire said, "I think — I think I believe you."

"What?"

"You've told me you didn't kill my husband. I think I believe you're telling me the truth."

"Do you," Bridger said. His voice skeptical, at best.

"I do. I'm not trying to trick you. I believe you."

"Well, you shouldn't. You don't even know me."

"I know what I feel. And if I'm a fool, then I'm a fool. They can tell me it doesn't make sense. But everything you've said makes sense. Everything you've done . . ."

"Because I haven't harmed you?"

"Maybe that's part of it."

He was shaking his head now. "Lady . . ."

"My name is Claire. Please don't talk to me as if I'm not someone."

"I'm not." He started to say something else, but then stopped. What would he have said? That he liked her? That she was a good-looking woman who seemed to have her head on straight? That she didn't deserve this either? What difference would it make?

He heard himself say, "There are people who want to kill you."

"Yes?"

"Do you know who they are?"

"I still don't." Claire said, "The people who told your friend about the coin collection, do you know who they were?"

"No. She wouldn't tell me."

"You think they're the same people who came after me?"

"Yeah. Probably." Bridger said, "I should have thought of it before."

"Sometimes it's hard to think clearly," Claire said.

"Yeah, sometimes."

And Claire was thinking of a woman named Maggie. Wondering what this mysterious woman looked like. Strawberry blonde with big boobs in a short print dress. Maybe a brunette with a short skirt who looked like she could play a secretary in one of those Stacy Keach *Mike Hammer* television shows. No matter how she imagined it, the woman was always tall. Had they slept together? Had she answered his phones and set up his appointments?

He was looking at her now.

And Claire was thinking, *Is he going to come over to me? What will I do if he crosses the distance and puts his hand on me? If he touches me on the shoulder and bends down . . .*

But he stayed where he was.

Bridger said, "I'm going to take you back now."

"What? What do you mean?"

"I'm going to take you back home. Or to the restaurant. Whichever you prefer."

THIRTY

It was not until they were on the road that Claire realized where they had been. The Kittatinny Mountain range, just a few miles from the Appalachian Trail, in a part of New Jersey that was green and rocky and far from the muck that was Newark and Secaucus.

They drove south on a twisty country road in the old Plymouth Fury convertible that Bridger had stolen. The car was a faded blue and the top was a faded white and they had the heater set high to compensate for the cold air making its way through the thin canvas roof. They were both quiet on that part of the drive, the only exchange between them being when Claire asked if she could turn on the radio and Bridger said she could.

They crossed the Delaware River at Phillipsburg then took Route 611 south. The road was narrow and lined by trees and towns with populations in the hundreds, the river still near them.

They were a few miles south of Easton when Claire spoke.

She said, "I don't think it's a good idea for you to take me to my house."

"Why not?"

"The police might be there."

He turned to her in the darkness and seemed to study her.

Claire did not look back at him. "They might be at the restaurant too," she said.

Bridger said, "Do you know what you're doing?"

Claire kept her eyes on the road. "Yes," she said.

Bridger sighed. It didn't make sense. Any of it. He had never met anyone like her before. He thought of Maggie and what she meant to him. But that was different.

Claire said, "Look, I can't explain it. I don't think I can, anyway. You've asked me to believe you and then you say you don't want me to. And I understand that. I do. Maybe you're a gifted con man and you've tricked me into thinking you're innocent. Innocent of murder, anyway. But then you've also told me that you've killed three men. And you haven't . . . you haven't harmed me. Shit, I don't know. We go through life thinking we have things figured out, but we don't. I'm not saying that I understand you or that I've figured you out. I haven't. But maybe I have."

"You —"

"No, let me finish. Please. I believe you because it feels right. It just . . . feels right. And I've trusted where I should not have trusted and I've been wrong. I've trusted in convention and it hasn't worked. And then this . . . I don't know. Maybe I believe you because it's easier to believe you than not believe you."

Bridger looked at the woman again. The pale skin of her neck set off against her dark hair.

He said, "What will you tell the police?"

She turned to him.

"What do you want me to tell them?"

For a moment he did not say anything. The road in front of them, illuminating in the headlights, "Helplessly Hoping" on the radio, the woman's legs pulled up on the car seat to keep warm.

"I don't know," Bridger said. "It's a crime to mislead the police."

"Three men abducted me and tried to kill me. You weren't one of them. I know that now. I plan to tell them about that."

"And how do you tell them how you got

out of there? How do you explain your escape?"

"I'll figure it out. Besides, I was unconscious when it happened. What could I tell them?"

"Tell them about how your husband was nervous when he heard about the guy being killed in South Philly. Maybe they'll connect it up and get this thing resolved."

"Maybe they will. What if they don't?"

"That's not your problem."

"It is my problem. Men tried to kill me, remember? Maybe you got what you need out of me. But I'm still involved in this."

"I know that, but —"

"Then why leave me out of it?"

"I'm not trying to do that."

"Men murdered my husband and tried to kill me. If the police are focused on you, I won't be safe. It isn't just about you."

"I know that," Bridger said. He was repeating himself now. This woman had him repeating himself. He looked at her again. Christ. Did she have to look like that? Beautiful and tough and keeping her shit together at a time like this. How often do you meet someone like this? He had chosen the life he had chosen and up till now he had no regrets, notwithstanding the events of the last couple of days. He had made his bargain.

But the woman was not part of that bargain. Professional criminals did not get to take up with beautiful, nice women who married judges and owned restaurants with French names. It was the way it was.

"I know," he said again. "Maybe . . . you could tell them about the guys who abducted you. Tell them where they can be found."

"Yes?"

"If they're still there, if no one's gone back to bury them or retrieve them, the police will be able to identify them. And maybe find out who they're associated with. Who they're working for."

"And then let you know?"

"Yeah."

In the darkness, Claire gave it some thought.

"It could work," she said.

The way she said it, cool and thought out, it made Bridger think about her again.

Claire said, "I could call you."

Bridger shook his head. "No," he said. "I don't have a cell phone. They can track cell phones. And I've got to get rid of this car. And . . . look, we can't do this."

"We can. No one would believe that I'm in contact with you. That's our advantage.

No one would believe it."

"I'm not sure I believe it."

She was smiling at him. "You see? That's why it'll work."

"Claire," he said, "you're going to get in over your head."

"No, you're wrong. I *was* in over my head. Not anymore."

An hour and a half later, they were in the parking lot of a convenience store near King of Prussia. Well lit and with phone booths.

Bridger said, "Have you got money?"

She checked herself.

"No. I must have lost my purse earlier."

Bridger handed her a couple of twenties. He said, "I'll call the restaurant tomorrow after five. I'll say I'm Mike Cremin, an old friend."

"Yeah, I'll remember. Hopefully, I'll have something for you."

Claire looked at him briefly. Then she scooted toward the passenger door. "I'll see you," she said.

Then she was out the door.

Bridger watched her until she was in the safety of the store, by the magazine stand, in view of the clerk.

Then he drove away.

THIRTY-ONE

What had a friend told her in college? Something like, it's not a lie if you believe it. Probably something she got off *Friends.* The key was, tell *mostly* the truth. Or, make sure what you're actually saying is true.

Bridger had told her it was a crime to lie to the police. Was that true? Was that what got Martha Stewart in trouble? She could have kept her mouth shut, pleaded the Fifth, and that would have been that. But she did talk and, in talking, tried to take them down a path that was not . . . quite . . . right. Tried to steer them away from the truth. And they didn't like that.

Claire Laval had never been a player. She ran her business honestly and paid all the taxes she was supposed to pay. There was no dealing under the table at her place. None that she knew of, anyway.

But this was different. This, she believed, was a matter of survival.

Wasn't it?

Trooper Pierce was the one she called. She believed he would telephone Lytle for her and the two of them would pick her up together.

That's the way it happened. It took them about thirty minutes to get there and when they got out of their unmarked detective's car Rod Lytle put an arm around her, waiting for her to put an arm on his shoulder or something so he would feel justified in giving her a full hug. She didn't give him the opportunity.

Pierce kept his distance. He said, "I can't tell you what a relief it is to see you. We feared the worst. Can you give us a statement, tonight?" He paused. "I mean, unless you feel you need to go to a hospital or something."

"I don't," Claire said. "Thank you." She took a breath. "No, I think it's better we talk about this tonight, while it's still fresh on my mind. Is there someplace we can get some coffee?"

They went to a diner closer to the city, where Claire ordered some coffee and buttered toast. Pierce ordered an iced tea.

Claire said, "I was abducted behind my restaurant. Three men wearing ski masks put me in a van. They put something on my face that made me pass out. I think it was chloroform. That's all I remember about that part."

Lytle was doing the questioning now. He said, "They were wearing masks?"

"Yes."

"Can you describe them anyway? I mean, as best you can."

"Sort of. I mean, I saw them later without the masks."

"How?"

"I came to . . . in the woods, somewhere. It turned out to be Bucks County. They were — they were digging a grave for me. I guess they were going to kill me."

"Did you see them, then, when you woke up?"

Claire made a point of hesitating. "Yes," she said.

Pierce said, "What?"

"Yes, I saw them. But they were dead by then."

"Dead?"

"Yes, I think so."

"How?"

"Shot, I guess. One of them was under a van."

"*Under* the van?"

"Yes. The other two were shot, I think.

240

And he was there."

Pierce said, "Who was there?"

"Mr. Bridger."

"Oh, Jesus," Lytle said.

Pierce said, "What did he do?"

"He came over to me and said we should leave."

Lytle said, "He *asked* you?"

"Yes."

Lytle said it again. "He asked you."

"Yes."

Lytle said, "But what was he doing there?"

"I don't know," she said.

Pierce said, "And you went with him?"

"Yes."

Pierce said, "Is he the one that killed those three men?"

"I don't know."

Lytle said, "How could you not know?"

Claire shrugged. "I didn't see anything. I woke up after it was done."

Pierce said, "Where did you go?"

"He took me someplace up north. I was pretty shaken up. I didn't know what to think."

"He kidnapped you?" Lytle said.

"No. I'd like to say he did. But he didn't. I agreed to go with him."

Lytle said, "You agreed — why?"

"He got me out of there," she said. "I

don't know. I may have been in shock or something."

Lytle said, "Jesus, you didn't — you didn't spend the night with him, did you?"

"No," Claire said, taking offense in her tone. She kept her eyes on Lytle for a moment. "We stayed in the same cabin, but . . . well, I must have fainted or something. I didn't see him again until I woke up this morning."

Pierce said, "And then what?"

"We talked."

"You talked," Lytle said.

"Yes."

"About what?" Pierce said.

"He told me he didn't kill my husband. He told me that someone else did and was trying to frame him for it."

Lytle said, "He told you this."

"Yes."

The detectives looked at one another. And Claire thought, get it over with. She said, "He and I were not in on it together, if that's what you're thinking."

Pierce gave her a glance. "No one said that," he said.

"You were thinking it," Claire said. "He thought it too."

"Who did?" Pierce said.

"Bridger. He thought maybe I had my

242

husband killed. Or hired someone to do it and the person I hired framed Bridger for it."

Pierce said, "Okay. How about you?"

"What do you mean?"

Pierce said, "What do you say?"

"I didn't do that. I didn't even know my husband was having an affair."

Pierce said, "Did you get him to believe that?"

"I think so."

Pierce said, "You have to admit, Ms. Laval, it looks bad."

"What looks bad?"

"You disappear for approximately twenty-four hours and you're with the prime suspect in your husband's murder."

"It's nothing I planned," Claire said. "Look, if you doubt what I'm saying, have that spot in Bucks County checked out. Unless those men have been moved, they should still be there."

"Say they are," Lytle said, "that doesn't necessarily clear you."

Claire gave him the little girl look, then transformed it to the look of a business-woman. "Clear me?" she said. "Am I a suspect now? Because if I am, I think I'm going to need a lawyer."

The detectives exchanged looks again.

Pierce said, "If and when that's the case, we're obligated to read you your Miranda rights before we question you. And we haven't done that."

Claire said, "Are you going to?"

Pierce maintained eye contact with her. A gentle bear, but a bear nonetheless. He said, "I don't know yet. I don't know if you've been entirely straight with us."

"Maybe you should look into Bucks County," Claire said, "and see what you want to do after that. And I'm going to stay with a friend tonight, if you don't mind. I don't feel safe at my home anymore."

Pierce said, "We'll look into Bucks County. Right away."

Claire said, "Would you mind calling me in the morning? To let me know what you find out."

The bear's gaze slackened. A little. "No, I don't mind," Pierce said. "We'll call you in the morning."

Pierce turned to Lytle again. Lytle shrugged and made gestures with his hands. He turned to Claire and said, "Can we drop you off at your friend's?"

"I'd appreciate it," Claire said.

She rode in the back of the police car, staring out the window. The City. Home. It

244

hadn't changed since she left it. It was the same. It did not feel as if it should be the same, but it was. All these changes. The death of her husband. And, perhaps in a different way, the death of her marriage. It was a morbid thought and she wondered, vaguely, if she was betraying Joe in some way. Then she thought, no, that's what you *think* you should feel. Feeling it and thinking you should feel it were two different things. And here she had been calling Bridger a sociopath earlier.

She thought, *What is this? Is it just an attraction? I feel close to a man I've hardly known over the space of twenty-four hours and, just like that, I'm willing to question a marriage that lasted several years? Would it have been different if the guy had been physically repulsive? Would it have been different if he didn't handle coffee mugs with a touch that was so sure? Am I this superficial?* It wasn't right. But, it was right. Deep down, she knew now that Joe had not only kept a mistress hidden from her, but other things. His distress over hearing that a man had been killed. What was that about? It had not been mere grief. Joe himself had said he hardly knew the guy; that he'd only just met him. No, it wasn't grief. It was fear. She had known it that night, but had not said anything. She had told him she loved him, and he had said he loved her too. Their last words to each other, in a sense. And it had been a deceit on both their parts.

Claire said, "There's something I remembered."

From the front of the police car, Trooper Pierce said, "What?"

"There's something I remembered," Claire said. "The night before he was killed, my husband was upset about something."

"Yes?"

"A man in South Philly had been shot to death. My husband said he knew him. He seemed upset by it."

Pierce turned in his seat. "Do you remember the man's name?"

"No. Joe didn't say his name. But it happened the day before. In South Philly." Claire said, "Maybe it meant something."

Pierce said, "We'll check it out."

Maxine, her friend, cried while she hugged her and the detectives left the front door and went back to their car. Maxine, overcome by emotion that Claire was still alive and looking like she needed a hot bath and hadn't been molested or harmed. Maxine's husband Gil, nodding and smiling gently in the background.

Gil said, "Would you like some tea?"

"No," Claire said. "A drink. Vodka tonic, if you don't mind making one."

They left her alone in the living room while they went to the kitchen to get her her sedative. When they were gone, Claire let herself sag against the wall and let out a healthy sigh. *Well,* she told herself, *you're in it now. Up to your neck.*

THIRTY-TWO

At dawn, there were police vehicles all over the place. Bucks County deputies, state police, one car from a nearby small town and the PSP crime scene investigation guys, looking more like engineering students than Horatio Caine or babes who looked as if they gave up NBA cheerleading for police work.

If it had been left to Lytle, they would have come the next morning, but Pierce wanted to check it out as soon as they dropped off Hannon's wife at her friend's.

They got to the place she had directed them to when it was still dark and saw two dead bodies, shot to death. They managed to keep their food in their stomachs, but it wasn't easy because the bodies had been in the woods for a while and forest creatures had come by and taken a nibble here and there. They found the third corpse underneath the van lying on its side, but they couldn't get a complete look at him until the tow truck arrived and pulled the van off.

Wow-wee. A triple homicide. Right?

Yeah, but all three of the guys were armed, the one under the van still clutching a Mac-10 machine gun. Maybe it had been mutual combat. Or maybe the guys had shot each other. Though that didn't make much sense. More likely, a mutual combat.

None of the corpses had identification on them. So they suspected they were professionals who would either run or keep their mouths shut if caught. Outfit guys, no?

Well, maybe. But almost certainly from Philadelphia or New Jersey. Maybe New York.

"I think Philly," Pierce said.

He turned out to be right about that.

THIRTY-THREE

Lieutenant Russ Morrow used to stop by Estrich's every morning and get two donuts with his coffee. One glazed, one chocolate. Thirty-eight cents apiece and with a cup of coffee, it was still less than two dollars. A deal, considering you'd pay almost twice that if you went to Starbucks and got a pastry with your coffee. But the donuts added up, and his wife started to make comments about being married to another heavy-assed cop. She said that cops ate donuts because they *wanted* to get fat and it had something to do with an unconscious fear of dying, a desire to have more layers protecting them against bullets and paranoia and the stress of . . . something. Whatever. Still, they were making his stomach strain against his shirts. So he knocked off the donuts and started having buttered toast at home before he left, usually eating one piece in the kitchen, the second in his car as he backed out of the driveway. It made a difference and he dropped some weight. But he still went to Estrich's for his coffee. A ritual he needed.

Other Philly cops would go there too. Talk shop and try to avoid the beginning of shift, like it was a thing that could be avoided. Metro police, some state officers, but rarely any feds. The feds *liked* Starbucks.

So when Lieutenant Morrow saw Agent Adam Roarke at Estrich's, he thought the guy had wandered in there by mistake. He expected a curt FBI nod from him, nothing more, so was surprised when the guy walked straight up to him with a look of dismay and need and said, "I need to talk to you."

"Yeah?" Morrow said. "What's up?" Still on his guard with the fed.

"It's about the Morano case," Roarke said.

"What?"

The agent looked around to see if anyone was listening. In a crowded donut shop.

Roarke said, "There's some things we didn't tell you."

Russ Morrow seemed to look at the agent a second time. Nervous, but wanting to confess something.

Morrow said, "Where's your better half?"

"He's not here."

Morrow raised his brow.

Roarke said, "You want to talk or not?"

"Yeah," Morrow said, "we can talk."

They got back to Troop K headquarters sometime that afternoon. Lytle slept in the passenger seat during the drive back and Pierce managed to get forty-five minutes on a cot before the woman came in. Pierce brushed his teeth in the men's room and they talked with her in an interrogation room.

Showed her photographs of three men:

Jeffrey Ray Gist

Kenneth Thomas Doolin

Gary Trent

Lytle said, "Do you know them?"

"No," Claire said. "I mean, they were wearing masks."

Lytle said, "These were the three dead men we found in Bucks County. They've got records. Armed robbery, assault with a deadly weapon, that sort of thing. Dangerous men."

"That's what I thought," Claire said.

Pierce said, "And you don't know them?"

"No," Claire said. "I'd never seen them before that night."

"You sure?" Pierce said.

"Yes. I'm sure."

Pierce said, "What about your husband?"

"What do you mean?"

Lytle said, "Did your husband know them?"

She almost said, *how should I know?* But stopped herself. "I don't know," she said. "If he did, he didn't tell me. Why?"

Pierce said, "You told us your husband was upset or bothered by someone being killed on the southside. Do you remember that man's name?"

"No. He didn't say."

Pierce said, "He never said anything about a Vince Salvetti?"

"No, he —" Claire stopped again. And thought for a moment.

He had never said anything to her. But she had overheard him. Sometime, some-place. She had overheard him saying "Vince" to someone. Claire tried to place it. It was like watching a movie on cable and seeing a not-so-famous actor in a small role and wondering where you had seen him before. More often than not, you had seen him do a guest role on *Seinfeld* or something like that. Working-class actors, looking for the next job, waiting to win the movie star lottery. Vince. Vincent. Where had she heard it?

On the telephone? Was that it? On the telephone behind the bar, using the telephone? Something like, "Okay, Vince." Had that been it?

Okay, what?

"What?" It was Pierce talking to her.

"What?"

Pierce said, "You stopped there. What is it?"

Claire said, "I remember him saying 'Okay, Vince' to someone on the telephone."

"When?"

"I don't know, exactly. Maybe a few weeks ago."

Lytle said, "What were they talking about?"

"I don't know. I just remember that he was . . . smiling. Or laughing."

Pierce said, "Like he was familiar with him?"

"Yes."

Pierce looked at Lytle for a few moments. Then turned back to Claire. He said, "Vince Salvetti, if this was the same man, was associated with Kenny Doolin. Or Kenny D, as he was known."

"Oh —"

"Only," Pierce said, "he wasn't. What I mean is, Vince Salvetti was not his real name. His real name was John Morano. And he was an FBI agent, working undercover."

Claire said, "I don't understand."

Lytle said, "We think Salvetti or Morano was involved with something with your husband. We're not sure what it is, yet. But . . . we're working on it."

Pierce said, "Did Bridger know your husband?"

"No."

"How do you know?" Lytle said. "How do you know he didn't know him?"

"I — I guess I don't. I mean, he didn't say he knew him."

Lytle said, "Would you have expected him to?"

"Yes," Claire said, not even thinking about it.

"*Yes?*" Lytle said. "Yes? The man's a professional criminal. You trust *his* word?"

"I just don't think . . ."

"You don't think what?" Lytle said.

"I just don't think he's a killer."

"He killed three people that you know of," Lytle said. "Why not your husband too? Just what did he do to you up there?"

Claire flushed. She said, "He didn't do anything to me. If he had, I'd've told you. I assure you that."

Pierce said, in a tone different than Lytle's, "Ms. Laval. It seems we owe you an apology."

Claire took her attention off Lytle. "For

what?" she said.

"For suggesting that you . . . well, that you might have been involved in anything. It seems likely now that your husband was associated, in some way, with the Tessa crime family. The Philadelphia branch of the Tessa Family. Are you familiar with them?"

"No."

Pierce said, "They were being investigated, infiltrated, by the Organized Crime section of the FBI. Your husband was involved somehow. Perhaps even a target of the investigation."

". . . a target? What does that mean?"

Pierce said, "It means the FBI may have been building a case against him."

"Against Joe? For what?"

"We're not sure. Yet. Perhaps racketeering. Perhaps for accepting bribes. The case was in process at the time of his death."

"The point is," Lytle said, "there is reason to believe the Tessas were onto him. That's why they killed the FBI agent and then him. We have evidence that the Tessas sent a couple of black males to kill Mr. Morano. That is, third parties. And we believe that Bridger was another one of those third parties sent to kill your husband."

"But . . . he saved me."

"From who?" Lytle said. "Those three

256

guys in Bucks County? Did it ever occur to you that that had nothing to do with you? That he killed those guys because they could be witnesses against him? Or because he thought they crossed him? Had you considered those alternative possibilities?"

There was a silence.

And Pierce said, "Have you?"

"No," Claire said. And wanted to add, *but he could have killed me too.* There was nothing to stop him from killing her as well.

But she didn't want to fence with these men anymore. Not right now. It was too much. Joe involved with organized crime? Another thing she'd known nothing about. How dumb was she? Just how gullible was she? Was it something *he* had seen in her? Something he had sensed? Take her up to a cabin in New Jersey and tell her anything. She'll believe it.

Lytle said, "You're not safe, Claire. Do you understand that now?"

". . . yes."

"You can go back to your friend's house again to stay the night," Lytle said. "We can't really order you not to. But we don't think you're safe there either."

"What then?"

"Well . . ." Lytle made a point of looking at Pierce, then said, "You can go to a hotel.

257

Or you can go to your house. Harold and I will take shifts watching over you."

Oh . . . no, Claire thought. "You mean," she said, "through the night?"

"Yes," Pierce said. "At least for a while. Until Bridger's caught."

Claire said, "But what about the others?"

Lytle said, "Others?"

"Other people working for the . . ."

"The Tessas?" Pierce said.

"Yes."

Lytle said, "You mean the ones in Bucks County? Well, you don't have to worry about them anymore."

Jesus, Claire thought. "Yes, I understand that. But won't the Tessas send others after them?"

"We don't know yet," Lytle said.

"Okay," Claire said. Okay. She said, "Which one of you goes first?" She waited for the answer she knew was coming. Lytle said, "Well, I guess I can do it tonight."

Claire said, "Will you pick me up at the restaurant tonight?"

"Yeah," Lytle said, "we can do it that way."

THIRTY-FOUR

Driving back to her restaurant, Claire was playing that last bit back. *Yeah, we can do it that way.* God, they were a *we* now. Angry now at a lot of people: Bridger, the horny cop, her deceased husband, herself. Not necessarily in that order.

But it was easier to start with Joe. Her unjustly murdered husband, her mother-in-law's son. Smiling Joe Hannon, friend of the everyman. Joltin' Joe . . . Claire thinking, *What have you done to me, you dumb son of a bitch?* Joltin' Joe has left and gone away and . . . left her in this massive fucking mess.

God, could he be so stupid to have gotten himself mixed up with mobsters? Could she have been so stupid not to have seen it? Not even seen any of it?

What was it he had used to say? Something like, "It isn't what you are, it's what projects." Ha ha. A clever politician's line.

Oh, so clever. So glib. Ha ha ha . . . dumb shit.

If he were here now, she could unload on him and tell him he would get divorce papers in the mail no later than Friday. Tell him he could pack his shit and get out of her house and go live with his idiot mother. But he wasn't here, he was dead and what was she supposed to do now? Go over to the cemetery and kick his tombstone over?

Three men in masks grabbing her and putting chloroform on her face and taking her up to Bucks County to kill her. *To bury her.* This was the situation he had put her in.

And none of it was in her control. She felt like a pinball, bounced around from Joe to mobsters to cops to a professional thief and then back around again, praying she wouldn't go down the hole. Joe getting her in this shit, then leaving her with it, men taking her up to the woods to bury her, a thief keeping her captive, and now a lonely, married cop wanting to stay the night in her home . . . she pictured that now, the man sitting on her sofa with his jacket off, watching her television. "Could I have a beer or an iced tea, if it's not too much trouble?" Christ.

She pulled her car into the parking lot of

Frères-Laval. Killed the engine of her Saab and looked at the sign again. *Frères-Laval.* Her place, her business. Hers before she married, hers as a widow. Hers. She ran it well. Perhaps even better than her father had.

But none of it meant anything to these fuckers. Thieves, mobsters, cops. Just another girl in distress. Just sit tight, little lady; we'll get you through this.

Claire locked the car and went inside, straight to the office where she kept a small safe in the closet. There was a message on her desk. Mike Cremin, the name Bridger had said he'd use. There was a local number written underneath it.

A pay phone in a laundromat? A diner? A hotel?

She could call Trooper Lytle and give it to him right now. Trace the number and bring the man in and let the police deal with him.

Claire dialed the number. It rang four, five, then six times before someone picked up.

"Yeah?"

It was him.

Claire said, "It's me."

Bridger said, "It's almost six. You said you'd be there at five."

261

"I had appointments." She stopped and waited.

"Okay," Bridger said. "Did you find anything out?"

"Yes. Why don't we meet somewhere?"

"Okay."

"The Reading Terminal Market. At John Yi's fish stand in one hour."

"All right."

Claire hung up the phone. She returned to the safe, turned the dial left, right, then left again and opened it.

She took a short-barreled .38 revolver out. She opened the cylinder to make sure it was loaded. It was.

It had belonged to her father. He had kept it for emergencies that had never come about. He had told Claire about it and showed her how to use it. They had both kept it secret from her mother, who had the Eastern aversion to firearms. To Robert it had been a tool, not an idol to be worshipped or devil to be feared.

Claire put the gun in her purse.

She parked the Saab in the garage at Twelfth and Filbert and crossed the street to walk into Reading Terminal Market through the Eleventh Avenue entrance. Then she was in and surrounded by the muffled roar of thousands of shoppers amid the usual tourists. The smell of fresh-baked Amish goods in from Lancaster County, fruits and vegetables lined up in colorful rows that sloped toward the customers. Commerce, food, and wine. The things that motivated Claire to go to work every day.

She walked through crowds, past the Dutch country meats, until she got to John Yi's Fish Market, smelling it before she saw it. She stood in front of the stall, flounders lying on ice. But did not see Bridger. She checked her watch. She was on time and then some. She looked over to the seating area. He wasn't there either. She looked down the aisle to see if he was standing among all the people. An older couple moved around a younger couple pushing a baby's pram and she saw a flash of something in the distance.

Him?

Yeah, him.

Looking back at her now, about forty yards away, standing in front of the spice terminal. He gestured a direction with his head and started walking down the C aisle.

Claire started walking down the B aisle.

They kept pace with each other as various businesses interrupted their view. Seventh Avenue, then Sixth, then Fifth . . .

With each one, she wondered if he would disappear. Break to his right and bolt. She knew what he was thinking. That she had brought the police along. Indeed, she had expected him to think it. Whatever he was, he wasn't dumb.

Fourth Avenue.

He was still there. Neither hurrying, nor taking his time.

Third . . . Second, Wan's Seafood behind them now, the Reading Terminal Market running out and into the street.

Traffic going by, more crowds. After a moment she saw him.

He was coming toward her, looking at her briefly, then gesturing past her to the taxi stand. Telling her to walk in front of him.

She did so. And he kept pace again, this time behind her and she stopped when she got to the taxi stand. She turned around again to look for him. She didn't see him. But then felt a touch on her arm and turned to see him and he only said hello before he guided her into a cab and got in with her.

Then the cab was moving away from the terminal, a base fare of $2.90 already on the meter.

Bridger turned to her and said, "Long day, huh?" The way a boyfriend or husband would talk. *He was a performer,* Claire thought.

"Yes," Claire said. "It has been."

Bridger directed the driver to a gray, rundown lot about two miles away. He paid the man from the back of the cab, keeping his face in the shadows as best he could. The cabbie left them there and Bridger pointed to a Chevy Impala. She walked alongside him without saying anything, parted when she got in the passenger side.

Bridger started the engine.

Claire said, "You sure do steal a lot of cars, don't you?"

"Cars are easy," Bridger said.

He didn't say anything more until they got to someplace called the Red Carpet Motel near the northeast airport.

THIRTY-FIVE

Bridger opened the door of the hotel room, which was on the second floor, and let Claire go in before him. He closed the door behind him and watched her walk over to the desktop and turn on the lamp.

Bridger stayed near the door.

From the opposite side of the room, he said, "Would you take off your sweater, please."

Claire turned to look at him. He was not holding a gun now. Just standing there with his hands at his sides.

Claire was wearing a brown sweater and a skirt.

She said, "What?"

"Would you take off your sweater, please?"

Claire waited a moment, looking in his eyes briefly, then pulled her sweater over her head. She threw it on the bed. She stood there in her skirt and black lace brassiere, her skin pale underneath.

Bridger stayed where he was. He raised his right hand and made a turning motion with two fingers. Claire turned slowly around, facing him again when she was finished.

"Okay," Bridger said. "You can put it back on now."

"You don't trust anyone, do you?"

"I'm sorry," Bridger said. "You can put it back on now."

She stood there as she was, the sweater still on the bed. She said, "What about my purse? Have you thought that there might be a wire in there?"

"Yeah, maybe."

She stepped over to the table to get it, giving him another look, direct eye contact as she put both hands on it, then one in as she pulled the gun out, separating it from the purse before throwing the purse on the bed in front of him.

She was pointing the gun at him.

For a moment, neither one of them said anything. A woman without her top pointing a gun at him. A first, he imagined, for both of them.

Claire said, "Why don't you check the purse now."

"Okay," Bridger said. He picked it up and emptied the contents out on the bed. Felt the sides and bottom. "Okay," he said again, stepping back from the bed. Bridger said, "Well, do you want me to turn my back while you put your top back on?"

"A little late for that now."

"I told you I was sorry. You know I have to be careful. Besides, that's nothing I can't see on the beach."

"I don't go to the beach," Claire said. She gestured to the chair that was on his side of the bed. "Will you sit there, please?"

Bridger sat down.

Claire stepped forward and pulled her sweater off the bed. She pulled it over her head, sticking the gun through one of the armholes. Then she pulled the chair out from the desk and positioned it so that she could sit down.

Claire said, "I talked with the state police."

"Did you tell them about the three men?"

"Yes. They found them. They were still out there. They work for a Family, apparently."

"What family?"

"Don't you know?"

"No. Why would I?"

"The police seem to think you would."

"Why?"

"They think you were hired by the Family to kill my husband."

"What family, Claire?"

"The Tessa crime family. That's what they told me, anyway."

"The Tessas? You mean, out of New York?"

"Yes."

Bridger didn't say anything for a moment. The woman with the gun in her hand was not on his mind then. He said, "Nick Blanco."

"What?" Claire said. "What did you say?"

"Nick Blanco. He runs the Philadelphia branch of the Tessas. Did they say anything about him?"

"I don't remember them saying anything about him."

"Why not?"

"Why not . . . what do you mean?"

"Why didn't they say anything about him?"

"I don't know. I can't read their thoughts. They seemed to be focusing on you, frankly."

"Why?"

"Because — because my husband was apparently mixed up with the Tessas. They didn't exactly explain how. Maybe he took money from them, maybe . . . he did something else. I don't know. He was being investigated by the FBI, and one of their undercover agents was killed. I mean, the undercover agent was killed the day before my husband. You know."

"I don't know. Tell me what happened."

"They think the Tessas found out about the undercover agent investigating my husband. So they killed him and then — had my husband killed so he couldn't testify against them. And they think the Tessas hired you to do it."

"Hired me to kill your husband?"

"Yes."

Bridger said, "And you believe that?"

"What do you want me to say?"

"You've got a gun in your hand. You can say whatever you like."

"And then what? Kill a human being in cold blood? We're not all like you, Mr. Bridger."

"You're more like me than you know."

"Shut up."

"Claire, if you think I killed him, kill me. Go ahead. If I didn't have it coming for that, I'd have it coming for being stupid."

"You don't make any sense."

"Claire, think about it. Ask yourself what makes sense. If I were hired by Blanco to murder your husband, would I have allowed you to live? Would I have questioned you in that cabin? Would I have agreed to see you again? You don't have to look into my soul

270

and ask whether I'm good or bad to figure that out."

"I've already figured out that you're not good. As to the rest . . . well you might have done all those things and still been guilty."

"Why?"

"Because you're twisted. Inside. Maybe you're in love with me."

"Yeah, maybe. But that doesn't make me twisted."

So it was out there now. Not terribly romantic, not terribly sweet. Just out there. And they were looking at each other, exposed now in a way they hadn't been before.

Claire said, "What do you want?"

"I told you what I want. I've always told you. I want to find out who killed Maggie. Who set me up for this," he said. "I think I've got it figured out now."

"You do?"

"Yeah." Bridger sighed. "And now that I have, I feel kind of stupid. It was right there in front of me all along."

Yeah, right in front of him. He should've known it was the outfit. They'd burn anybody. No honor among thieves. He had never met Nick Blanco, but he knew that Blanco ran the Philly branch of the Tessa's operations. And he knew that Maggie had been involved with Nick years ago. She'd never quite been his mistress. But he had probably been one of her customers back when she was hooking. For him, it would have been just another whore whose life didn't really matter. It was all A, B, and C now. Blanco had approached Maggie and told her about the coin collection and asked her to get in touch with mister professional, Daniel Bridger. Master thief and premier chump of Baltimore.

Claire said, "But why me?"

"Pardon?"

"Why do they want me, too?"

"Because they think you know something. Your husband must have been taking money from them. Maybe laundering it through your restaurant. Have you noticed any unusually large sums of cash coming in?"

"No," Claire said. *Joe must have been keeping it to himself,* she thought. Apparently even mobsters couldn't rely on him. Claire said, "I didn't know anything about it."

"I believe you," Bridger said. "But . . . it doesn't make any difference to them."

"But that's so barbaric. I didn't do anything."

"Well, neither did I. Neither did Maggie. It's just — objects to them."

"So, what? We just wait to die?"

"No. And I'm not waiting to get arrested either."

"Does this Nick Blanco know you?"

"No, not really. He knows of me. As he knows of you. It doesn't always have to be personal."

"But it *is* personal. He wants to snuff out our lives. It's very personal. I mean, don't you feel that way about your friend?"

"Don't ask me about that," he said. "That's my problem."

"I'm involved in this too, you know."

He saw that he had wounded her. And it stopped him for a moment. He pictured her again standing in front of him in her brassiere, the black lace contrasting with her smooth, pale skin.

"I know," he said.

Claire felt her heart beating. Alone in a motel room with a man who stole things for a living. Airplanes roaring overhead from time to time, the only light in the room coming from the lamp on the desk, in a universe now where time and place had somehow shifted.

She said, "Did you say a minute ago that you were in love with me?"

"I might've," Bridger said.

Her mouth quivering as she spoke, she said, ". . . but it doesn't make sense."

"Maybe it does."

"I asked you a minute ago what you wanted. And you never really answered me."

"Yes, I did."

She was shaking her head. "No, you didn't. Not really."

Bridger stood up. Stayed on his side of the bed.

He said, "It's up to you."

Claire put the gun on the desk. Then she stood up and walked around to his side of the bed.

Then she was standing in front of him, her hand resting lightly on his chest, as she started to lean in.

Bridger said, "Maybe we should turn the light off."

"You didn't offer to do that for me," Claire said.

THIRTY-SIX

After, the woman went to sleep. And then Bridger closed his eyes too. Opened them about fifteen minutes later to see the woman curled up in a fetal position next to him, her backside exposed. The same woman he had met no more than a couple of days ago. She was still sleeping. Bridger pulled the blankets up over the both of them.

She was something to look at. And not just look at. To be with and talk to, and sometimes just not to talk. He found himself thinking about her husband and the years he had had with her. Christ, in a crappy airport motel envying a dead man.

It was stupid. She was not someone who could be with him long term and he knew it. She would know it too if she thought about it. He sensed that, like him, she was a realist. There were paths and structures in this life; rules that had to be respected. To fight them was to fight nature and nature always won in the end.

What were the things that mattered to him? Not the things that should matter, but the things that did? He was past thinking about a wife and a family and a house in the suburbs. He doubted he ever had thought in those terms. Even when he was in prison. Cars, money, the next job, women more so than a woman. Maggie had mattered to him. He had probably wanted her as a girlfriend, maybe even as a wife. Maybe not. She had not allowed it to get that far, anyway. Never had given him and her a trial run. Maybe it would've worked.

Probably not, though. She was gone now and she would not want him to pretend that there was more to them than there had been. She was a realist, herself. Perhaps too much so.

And now there was this woman. Claire. Not Maggie, but Claire. A different woman altogether. He could tell himself that she reminded him of Maggie, but it would be a lie. She wasn't Maggie. She was someone else. She was different. Earlier, the wife of a dead spouse. Then, a kidnapping victim. Then, a woman with him in a cabin in the Kittatinny Mountains, sitting on a chair with her legs tucked up beneath her. Then, a woman standing in a black lace brassiere pointing a gun at him. Then, a lover in bed with him. Another woman during that time, naked in the dark, her face discernible but not so much. It could have been someone else then. A different woman making sounds of passion, saying things to him that were natural and not unladylike. Murmuring things, but not saying his name. Like it would be too much to acknowledge that it was him. It had been something.

A stranger, yet not a stranger. A woman who had not put up the barriers that Maggie had. Maggie was part of his world, and this woman was not. Yet Maggie had kept him out.

He wondered if it was fair to compare them. Not only as lovers, but as people. Maggie had had a hard life. Marriage to a gangster who had been stupid and gotten himself killed. Maybe Maggie's husband had deserved it. No, he probably had deserved it. Got cocky and mouthy and talkative and the outfit had to shut him down. Jack McGurn had known the rules. If he had forgotten them, that was his fault . . . maybe Maggie had broken a rule herself.

It would be easier for him if he could believe that. Believe that, hey, she fucked up and trusted the wrong people and it got her killed. Like swimming too far out in the ocean. A sad and tragic thing, but goddamnit, she should have known better. It would be nice to think so, because then maybe he could walk away from this and forget about it.

But it wouldn't work. He could spend all night trying to rationalize it, but it wouldn't work. Because Maggie didn't deserve it. It didn't matter how scared you were, Maggie did not deserve to have the life choked out of her.

Bridger had a few rules of his own. One of them was: never work with the outfit. They'll fuck you over for milk money. Kill you, rat you out to the cops, take your money and all that matters to you. The outfit with all their blood oaths and *omertas* and codes of silence and Joe Valachi's kiss of death and I'm better than you because I'm full Sicilian and you're only half-Sicilian and you put this much garlic and sugar in the sauce . . . all of it bullshit. Even the feds were surprised at how easily those fuckers would sell each other out. The thing to remember was, they just couldn't be trusted.

But they were savage and not to be taken lightly. Which supported another of Bridger's rules: when you see outfit, get out. Quietly, if possible. But quickly for sure.

Get out and get in the shadows and steal away.

Maggie had got him in. She probably hadn't meant to. She probably had been overconfident and not seen all the ways it could go wrong. But now it was done and he was in and maybe he had played a part in allowing that to happen. He had not picked a fight with them. They had picked one with him. Killed a friend of his and set him up for a lifetime prison sentence.

And they were the outfit. Not some group of second-rate jackboys. The outfit.

So the wise thing to do was get out. Quietly, quickly.

There should be no shame in running. Not from the Tessa Family. Not from guys who put people on hooks and giggled about it. Taking them on was like running headlong with a switchblade into troops manning machine guns.

He had enough money that he could go underground. Maybe leave the country and go to the Far East. Mob politics being what they were, maybe Nick Blanco would be dead in a few years, the casual victim of a takeover or change of the guard. And maybe then Bridger could come back home. If not, he could buy another identity and start all over again, continuing his lifestyle else-

where. Nick Blanco could have Philadelphia.

But then there was the woman. There was
Claire Laval.

And when he realized that, he realized he
didn't really have a choice. If he left, they
would kill her sooner or later . . . probably
sooner. The police would not be able to
protect her forever.

He looked at her again. Her face and
shoulders visible above the covers, her dark
hair falling over her eye. He looked at her
and he felt grateful to her. He felt grateful
because she had made the decision easier
for him.

When she awoke, he was dressed. Sitting in
the chair at the desktop. He was looking at
her when she awoke, but turned his head
away when he saw that she was up.

Claire said, "What time is it?"

"It's nine o'clock."

"Nine," she said. "I have to get back to
the restaurant."

"Yeah?"

"The police officer, the trooper, is picking
me up from work. He's supposed to escort
me home."

"Why?"

"He's protecting me. From you, apparently."

Bridger said, "Oh."

Claire said, "It's like I'm married. Sneaking around him."

Bridger smiled.

"It's strange, isn't it?" he said.

"Yes, it's very strange," she said. "Thank you, though."

"For what?"

"I don't know. Saving my life, I think."

"You believe that now?"

"I think I've always believed it."

They were both quiet again. The sound of distant aircraft again, trucks and cars driving on the freeway nearby.

Claire said, "What happens now?"

Bridger said, "I'm going to take care of it."

"How are you going to do that?"

"I'm not sure yet. I've got some ideas."

"I'll help you," Claire said.

"No. You've already helped. More than you should have."

"I told you, I have a stake in this too."

"I understand that." Bridger stood up. "I'll go outside while you get dressed."

"You don't have to do that," Claire said. "Nothing you haven't seen before." She smiled. "Or does the light hurt my image?"

"No," he said. He was looking at her again. Sitting up in bed with the sheets around her breasts, looking back at him but not saying anything. A direct look that he was fairly sure he understood. He walked over to her. "Not at all," he said.

Outside, the parking lot was almost bare. The Chevy they had come in, a couple of semi-trucks and not much else. The faint light could be detected in the second floor window. Then it went out.

In the car, she said, "What?"

"What?" he said.

"You were looking at me."

"Yeah. I was looking at your earrings, actually."

"My earrings?" She smiled. "Why would you look at those?"

"They're diamonds."

"You're going to steal them?"

"No. Did your husband give them to you?"

"No. I bought them. For myself. You like them?"

"Very much." Bridger said, "How much did you pay for them?"

She looked at him again. "About six hundred. Why? Do you think they're fakes?"

"No, they're real enough. Would you take two thousand dollars for them?"

"What? You want to buy them?"

"Yes."

"Why?"

"It's hard to explain. Will you sell them to me?"

"But I like them."

"You can buy two more pairs with two thousand dollars."

"I suppose I could, but . . . what do you have in mind?"

"It's better if you don't know. But . . . if you're asked about them later, tell them they've been missing. They've been missing for a while, but you haven't noticed because —"

"Because of all this stuff that's been going on?"

"Yes." Bridger said, "Do you have tissue in your purse?"

"I think so."

"Put them in the tissue and then put the tissue in my pocket." He looked at her in the dark. "Please?"

"You're paying me for these."

"Yeah." He took out a wad of bills.

"Just give me five hundred. Otherwise I'll feel like you're paying for something else."

She removed the earrings and put them in a tissue and put them in his pocket. She took the roll of twenties and put them in her purse. Neither one of them spoke of trust. She sought no further explanation.

Claire said, "You're a strange man."

When they got downtown, she told him to pull over. She said, "I don't think you should take me to my car. You might be seen."

"But —"

"I'll get a cab. Don't worry."

He did as she asked and pulled over. She turned and looked at him briefly. "Will you call me and let me know what happens?"

"I'll try."

She touched his hand, but did not lean in to kiss him.

"Good luck," she said. And was gone.

THIRTY-SEVEN

Bridger walked into the diner carrying a stuffed teddy bear. It was a big one — the sort you might win at a state fair — and it had a Philadelphia Eagles jersey on it. He nodded to the lady behind the counter who didn't nod back as he came around and went straight through the kitchen and then up the stairs.

The big black guy that was standing at the top of the landing gave him one of those are you kidding me expressions and Bridger said, "It's for my girlfriend. She's playing cards in there."

"Get the fuck out of here," the man said.

"But —"

The man pointed down the stairs.

"Go. *Now.*"

Bridger took him in. A big fucker with a lot of weight above the belt. But that could work in your favor. Particularly when they leaned forward. He had a look in his eyes that said he liked to hurt people, picturing the opportunity to give the big mouth a clean pop on the chin and send him and his teddy bear tumbling down the stairs.

He needed a little motivation, though.

Bridger said, "Come on, man, it's her birthday. Whaddaya got to be such a prick for?"

And saw the black guy smile.

That would suffice.

The guy leaned forward and threw a right as Bridger dropped the bear, let the guy commit himself and put his weight on his left leg as he was getting ready to follow through and Bridger stepped in and kicked that left kneecap in.

He heard it pop and then the man was on the ground starting to scream but then Bridger was on top of him, covering his mouth with his hand. He took a pistol out of the guy's leather jacket and put it in his own pocket. Then Bridger showed him his own .45, the barrel extended with a black silencer. Bridger gestured to the man's good knee.

Bridger said, "You want to keep the other one? You can if you get that door open and cooperate."

There were two armed men on the other side of the door. They heard the familiar four raps and one of the men walked over and opened it up and was hit in the face with Bridger's gun. He went down, blood pouring from his nose. And then the other man was reaching inside his jacket but Bridger was pointing the .45 in his face, only a few feet away.

"Don't," Bridger said. "Don't do that. Put your hands on your head."

The man hesitated.

Bridger said, "I'll count to three. I reach three, you die. One, two — good. Now get on your knees."

The man did so. Bridger saw a young cocktail waitress. "You," he said. "Take his gun and his and bring them over here. Don't get in front of him."

When she was done with that, Bridger pulled two pairs of handcuffs out of his coat pocket and told her to handcuff the black guy and the bloody nose together, back-to-back. She did so and Bridger told everyone to lie down on the ground, stomachs touching the floor.

"You," Bridger said to the guy on his knees. "Get up."

The man got up and Bridger motioned for him to take him back to the office. Bridger said to the girl and everyone else, "I come out of that office and I see anyone standing or sitting, I'll kill 'em. No exceptions." He said to the man who had been on his knees, "Let's go."

They got to the office door and Bridger shoved the back of the man's head, put his body behind it and broke the door open. The man's body fell over the desk, knocking over containers of Chinese takeout, a bald guy behind the desk in a white shirt and tie standing up, saying, "What the fuck?"

Bridger said, "Where's Nick?"

"Nick ain't here," the bald guy said. "Who the fuck're you?"

"I'm the man taking the bank. Where is it?"

"Where is what?" the bald man said.

"The bank that's funding those chips out there. That's what I came here for."

"You gotta be fucking crazy, you think I'm —"

The white coffee cup on the desk exploded, the forty-five bullet having left the silenced barrel.

"You see that?" Bridger said. "The next one goes in your thigh. It'll bleed out, but you'll live long enough to get the money out of the safe and give it to me. Now move."

The bald guy pointed to a wooden chest

against the wall. "The safe's in there."

"You got heat in there?"

"No."

"Good. It's not worth dying for."

The bald man was looking at the barrel of the .45, agreeing. He took stacks of bills out of the safe and set them on the floor. Bridger took a blue plastic shopping bag out of his pocket and threw it on the floor.

"Put it in that," he said.

The bald guy did so, but he hadn't lost all his nerve. He looked up while he was doing it and said, "I don't think you know what you're getting into, pal."

"Right," Bridger said. "Get over there by him . . . good." He backed away to the open door. Looked out briefly at the people lying on the floor. He turned back to the bald guy.

"You tell Nick, this is just a down payment."

"For what?"

"He knows," Bridger said. He looked at the yellow cell phone clipped to the man's waist. Bridger said, "Give me your phone."

The man slid it over and Bridger said, "Tell him he can call me on your line. And we'll discuss it. Otherwise, I'll put him out of business."

"There's almost seventy thousand dollars

289

in that bag," the bald man said. "How much more do you think he owes you?"

"About another seven hundred and thirty," Bridger said. "Tell him that too."

THIRTY-EIGHT

"Fuckin' a," Blanco said, "you mind telling me what I'm paying these guys for?"

Maddox said, "He busted Amon's knee. That happens, you can't even stand."

"What am I fucking running here?" Blanco said. "The fucking Ice Capades? Huh? A man comes up the stairs, you keep him out. I mean, what am I paying these guys for?"

Maddox mentally sighed to himself. It was no use trying to talk reason to Nick when he was like this. Not listening and saying the same shit over and over. Pissed off and maybe a little bit scared too. D'Andrea would find out about it and let the both of them know the Tessas were displeased and in need of a very good explanation. Seventy thousand was milk money to them, but a man had come in to one of their operations, by himself no less, scared the clientele and walked out without a scratch. The man someone Nick had crossed and underestimated.

Maddox had been there when Arnold had told them what the man said. That Nick owed him another seven hundred grand and change and Nick would know what he was talking about.

Nick did know, but he could tell by the look on Maddox's face that Maddox didn't so he would have to explain it. Nick said, "I told that fucking Chan whore that there was a four-million-dollar coin collection in Hannon's house and I would help her get twenty percent on it. That's eight hundred grand. Fucking whore, she bought it."

"But there never was a coin collection," Maddox said. "Is this guy so fucking stupid, he hasn't figured that out yet?"

"Of course he's figured it out. Jesus. Don't you see, Claude? He's holding me to a contract I made with the woman. Telling me I'm bound by it, no matter what."

"I don't understand," Maddox said.

"Yeah? I do," Nick Blanco said. He was through explaining it to Claude.

Maddox said, "So, what then? You're just supposed to give it to him out of your own pocket?"

Or the outfit's, Nick thought. Do that and Henry D'Andrea would be down here in a flash. Accompanied by about twenty mooks armed with shotguns and shovels. They'd make him dig his own grave or have it dug already when they took him out to the woods so he could have a good look at it before they put a couple of caps in his skull. Or beat him to death. Probably the latter; he'd been disrespectful to Henry last time he'd seen him and Henry would remember it. These guys were all about remembering. And after he was gone, his wife would receive the typical backhanded words of sympathy. Nick was a good guy, but this was what happened to guys who screwed up and couldn't mind their own store. With great power comes great responsibility and all that shit.

As it was now, Nick thought he was probably personally on the hook for the seventy grand Bridger had taken from the poker bank. A penalty fine. It didn't do much damage to him financially, but the damage to his image was something that couldn't be shrugged off. Nick Blanco's operation was hit by some independent; knees were broken and noses were busted open, money stolen and before the guy left he made it clear that it was about him. *You tell Nick, this is just a down payment.* He could tell Arnold to keep that shit to himself, but if he did, Arnold

would know that Bridger had spooked him
and he couldn't have that. He couldn't have
it.

Everybody watching him now, wondering
what he would do. Nick Blanco who always
kept it together. Handsome Nick, the cool
customer whose shirts were never stained
with perspiration. Watcha gonna do now,
Nick?

He said to Maddox, "D'Andrea doesn't
know about this, does he?"

"No, I didn't tell him."

"I don't mind if you did, Claude. It's just
that he'd overreact and think he'd need to
get involved."

". . . okay."

"We'll handle it."

Maddox said, "I can take care of it."

Nick Blanco shook his head. "All respect,
Claude, this ain't like that thing you handled
before. Those guys were punks who more
or less left a trail of bread crumbs led to
their doorstep. I don't think you're going to
be able to find this guy."

Maddox remembered it being more complicated than that, but he was expected to
keep his mouth shut at certain times. He
said, "What then?"

"He's not getting any more money."

"No."

"But — we have to let him think he is. He's desperate. This thing here proves it. The police are after him and he wants us to give him traveling money so he can leave the country. He's not thinking straight."

Maddox didn't say anything.

And Nick said, "So . . . we call him. Offer him something. If we offer to give him — what was it he said?"

"Seven hundred and thirty thousand."

"If we offer to give him that, he'll know we're lying. We have to offer him a figure he can believe in. Say, a hundred. Maybe a hundred and fifty. We tell him that and maybe he'll agree to meet with us."

Maddox was nodding. He said, "And he gets to keep the seventy. With a hundred and fifty added to that, he'd clear over two hundred. He'll tell himself he can live with that."

"He'd be a fucking fool not to," Nick said. "Maggie Chan isn't worth dying for."

Bridger was sitting in a car parked in an A&W drive-in. He pressed the red button and ordered a cheeseburger and a cup of coffee. The voice on the box asked him if he wanted fries with that and he said no he wouldn't.

He leaned back and put his head against

the headrest and closed his eyes. The window was open and he felt the cool breeze on his face and it made him feel better. Seventy grand in his pockets and if the cops happened to find him here he might offer to give them all of it instead of starting the car and trying to escape. He used to carry five thousand with him on most of his jobs in case he ran into something like that. It had only become necessary once, after a job in Louisville. It was during the holiday season and he imagined there were a lot of presents under the cop's family Christmas tree that year. Of course, he wasn't wanted for murder then. Still, he smiled when he remembered the look on that patrolman's face when Bridger handed him the money and the way the earnest young cop had said, "Thank *you,* sir," like he was taking money for the Salvation Army. Southern gentility.

The cell phone rang.

Bridger took it out and answered it.

"Yeah," he said.

"Hey," a voice said.

Bridger said, "Who am I speaking to?"

"You know who," Nick said. "I understand you're looking for me."

"That's right."

"Something about me owing you money?"

"Yep."

"You mind explaining why?"

Bridger said, "I'm not asking, if that's what you're getting at."

Nick Blanco laughed. "Man," he said. "You got a lot of salt for a guy on a phone. But you're not very fucking bright. I got two guys here with injuries'd like to have a word with you."

"Get to it, Nick. You can pay me what you owe me or you can get hit again. It's up to you."

"Listen, pally, let's get something straight: you hit *one* of my places and you got lucky. That's all. This professional bullshit *attitude* you have about yourself, you can save that shit for the fucking mirror. You're a fucking temporary nuisance to me, nothing more. But, it just so happens I'm feeling generous today. So I'm going to make you an offer."

"What's that?"

"I'll give you a hundred grand and you get out of town. Go back to Baltimore and get the fuck out of my face."

Bridger hesitated. Then he said, "I'm going to need more than that."

"I don't give a shit what you need. This is a one-day offer. Tomorrow it's off the table and soon you will be too."

Bridger debated it, but went ahead and asked it anyway. "You think you owe me anything?"

"No, I don't," Nick said. "You and Maggie got greedy and you walked right into it. That's your fault, Dan. You of all people should know what it costs to be stupid. If you were smarter, you'd've seen it. But you didn't."

"No," Bridger said. "I didn't."

"It's a harsh fucking world, Dan. You know that and Maggie knew it too. But . . . like I said, I want this thing resolved."

"It's not enough for what you did to her."

"We deal in reality, Daniel. Not what someone deserves or doesn't deserve. You know how it is. Don't you?"

"Yeah."

"Then you know I'm being generous here."

The carhop walked up and set his cheeseburger and coffee on the tray that was attached to the car window. Bridger gave her a tenner and waved her off. He took a bite of the cheeseburger, chewed then swallowed.

Bridger said, "How soon can you get it to me?"

THIRTY-NINE

It turned out Claire's fears were justified. As she had predicted, Lytle was treating the assignment as some sort of domestic arrangement between them. *Let's just live together for now and if it works out, hey, we'll get married.* God help us. When he had picked her up from the restaurant, he had actually said, "So how was your day?" Oh, too familiar. Way too familiar. And that was just the start.

And how, pray tell, should she answer *that? Fine, honey. I had sex with your chief suspect in a cheap hotel room. Twice.*

Tell him *that* if he has need of news.

Bridger had told her to keep the gun in her purse. He had said he was going to take care of things but if he didn't succeed, she might still need to protect herself.

Claire had said, "But the police said they'll protect me."

And Bridger had looked back at her

without saying anything for a moment. Like she was simple-minded or something. It was enough to irritate her, but then he said, "Just keep it with you, for me. Please?" And that changed things for her.

It shouldn't have made sense, that. A professional thief telling her to keep her own gun, for him, and she had accepted the gesture as if it were some sort of valentine. But this time, she just accepted it. She was past the point now of wondering about her sanity, wondering anymore whether she should do things that made sense. Because he made sense. In this time, in this place, he made sense to her. It was not something she would ever be able to explain to even her closest friends, yet alone a cop. But that didn't matter because she had come to terms with it herself and that was good enough.

Bridger had said that if she saw guys rushing her again, from a van or a car, she was to pull the .38 out and shoot the closest one in the chest. Odds were, after that, the rest would scatter. He said, "Don't pull that thing out and warn them or ask them to stop. Just shoot. They're not going to believe you'll do it until it's been done."

Claire said, "Is that what you would do? Just shoot without warning?"

"Maybe," he said. "But I'm not you. They'd believe me."

"Yes," she said. "They would."

And Bridger said, "No one said it was fair." And left it at that.

Now, when Trooper Lytle asked her how her day was, Claire hesitated not at all to say that it had been uneventful. It was only later, when she was alone in her bedroom, that she paused to ask herself if this lying business was coming a little too easily to her. But she didn't spend much time answering herself.

In the car, driving back from the restaurant, Lytle said, "So . . . you want to catch some dinner?"

"Oh, no thanks," Claire said. "It's late and I already had dinner. There's things in the refrigerator though if you're hungry." She made her voice pleasant. A professional sort of pleasant. Polite, though not giving any sign that things were going to warm up. It made her feel bad. A little bad. Being snobby like this. But men like this forced her to be remote.

At the house, she almost felt sorry for him. She could see he was uncomfortable as she unlocked the door. A boy on the porch, wondering if he was going to get a kiss goodnight and maybe something more. Lifting up one foot and then the other . . .

Then they were in the house and in the kitchen and Lytle said, "Well . . ." and Claire thought, *that is that.*

She said, "Well, I'm going to sleep. If you want anything from the kitchen, help yourself. I'll see you in the morning."

He still had his jacket on when she went up the stairs. *A little bewildered,* she thought, *but it's not my problem.* Besides, the bastard *was* married.

Trooper Lytle made himself a sandwich, using the hoity-toity's special bread that you had to cut slices from yourself. No Wonder here, by God. *Bitch,* he thought. Probably looking for another lawyer. Or a doctor. Lytle found the television and saw that they had cable. He found the ESPN channel and it made him feel better.

FORTY

Nick gave Maddox the go-ahead to line up a crew of about a dozen men. He told Maddox the man needed to die, but how he got it done was up to him. Nick Blanco was not a micromanager by nature, and he was aware that Maddox had more of the hunter's instinct than he did. He also sensed that Maddox was a little sore at him for giving Kenny D the job on Hannon's wife. Maddox hadn't said anything that could be construed as critical about it. Hadn't even implied that Kenny had fucked up. Who was to say it would have gone any different if Maddox had been there? Still, there was no denying that Maddox was the better planner. Particularly when it came to hits.

All of the men they had gathered were Nicky's boys. Some of them young, some of them in their middle years. Nick told Maddox he had a date with his wife and that Maddox was to take care of it and call him when it was done.

Then Maddox was with the crew of a dozen, telling them where they needed to be and when they needed to be there. It was going okay and Maddox kept control when one of the younger ones decided to show the others how big his balls were.

It was one of these punks with a shaved head who called himself Marlon. He said, "If you've got the guy coming here, why not just open up on him when he gets there? I mean, when he gets within range?"

Maddox paused and did not look at the kid when he responded. Maddox said, "What?"

The one called Marlon said, "I said, why don't we just open up on the piece-a-shit when he gets there."

Then Maddox looked at him, resting his eyes on the guy in an unflattering appraisal before he answered.

Maddox said, "This guy's not stupid. He sees you out front of the hotel, he'll drive off."

"You fill that windshield with rounds," Marlon said, "he won't get far." He laughed at himself then, waited for someone to join him. Maybe one guy did, but that wasn't enough.

Maddox said to someone else, "Who is

304

this?" Pointing his finger at the punk, but not giving him eye contact.

One of the older guys said, "His name's Marlon. He's Jimmy's cousin. He's okay, Claude. He's just young."

Maddox looked at Marlon directly and Marlon found himself shifting his feet in the presence of a man who looked like he would have no more trouble shooting him than he would a pheasant.

"Anything else?" Maddox said.

"No, Mr. Maddox."

Maddox held his stare on him a little while longer until Marlon put his eyes on the ground. The point made.

But another one lost on the younger man. *Punk,* Maddox thought. You give some of these younger mooks a weapon, and they think all of a sudden they know things. But they don't. You track your prey, but you don't chase him. Not without thought. Usually, they'll just outrun you. Maybe because they're faster and maybe because they've got the advantage of wanting to survive. These things required patience. You had to wait and let them walk into the trap you've set.

Once Bridger was in the hotel, the exits would be closed off. Sealed. Not before. You could try to explain it to young mooks who talked of firing machine guns into fleeing cars, but they probably wouldn't listen.

The name of the place was the Graystone Hotel. It was in Center City. A nine-story hotel with a torn red awning, the iron frame partially exposed like a skeleton. A handful of vagrants occupying the first and second floors, the ones above more or less empty.

It was the place where Nick Blanco had said he would deliver the money.

From a distance of three blocks, Bridger looked at it. A brownstone building, calling itself gray. Named, probably, between the First and Second World War. Maybe a nice hotel way back when, though probably not.

Blanco had told him a man would meet him in room 810. The eighth floor. Maybe they'd push him out of a window from up there. Maybe they'd just shoot him and leave him up there to be eaten by rats, months going by before anyone found his corpse. Maybe they'd packed the whole goddamn building with dynamite and they would just blow it up once he got in there.

The way Blanco had talked, maybe *he* believed that *Bridger* believed he was going to be paid. *Maybe,* Bridger thought. If so, it could give him a bit of an advantage in this. Maybe. But what difference did it make, he would have to go in anyway.

Bridger drove away from the hotel.

At the art museum, he found what he needed.

When he first heard the siren, Maddox thought it was the police. Or a fire engine. *Christ.* Then realized it was a . . . Christ, a fucking car alarm. Piercing the night.

It will stop, Maddox thought.

But it didn't. It just kept fucking going.

Shit.

Well, he thought, he couldn't leave this room. Someone downstairs would have to do something about it.

There were three men posted in the hallway on the first floor and a couple more in the alleyway. The car alarm kept going and they all made their way to the front of the hotel and when they got to the front they saw what it was.

A Corvette, its lights flashing and alarm whooping like a son-of-a-bitch, and Maddox was buzzing one of them on his walkie-talkie and saying, *"Turn that fucking thing off."*

They got to the Corvette and one of the men managed to disarm it.

No one in the car, though. Or near it.

■ ■ ■ ■

The men's backs were about twenty yards from him when he jumped up and grabbed the fire escape ladder. It stayed where it was and didn't creak like he feared it would. Bridger got in the window in the second floor and was in the hotel before they got back.

He was in a room. A bed without a mattress in one corner. Not much else. He looked to the sides. Double doors. Access to the adjoining rooms. *Okay,* he thought. *Okay.*

He went to the door to the hallway and opened it silently. Peered out. No one. He went to the stairwell and stood in it before going up or down. Listened.

Voices from below.

He listened closer.

Murmurs, sober conversation. He couldn't make out the words, but he could detect enough to know it wasn't the conversation of vagrants.

He moved to the side of the wall, then began climbing the stairs, his steps quiet.

He got to the landing of the third floor. He moved out of the stairwell and into the hallway. He looked down the hall. Nobody.

But then heard something. Movement.

Coming from near him. A door up on the right.

Bridger moved further down the hall. He heard a toilet flush. He got to the side of the bathroom door and flattened himself against the wall. He heard footsteps, a body moving, not shuffling, but moving as an able man moves and the door swung open.

Bridger grabbed the man by the front of his jacket with his left hand, holding him steady for a moment, as he brought the butt of his .45 down on the guy's head and knocked him unconscious.

Bridger dragged him back in the bathroom, where he could see the man in a faint yellow light. A tough guy, wearing good clothes. Bridger took a gun out of the guy's jacket. No vagrant here. He dragged the man into the last stall and left him there.

Well, he thought. There were men out front and on the sides. And now men in the building. He could leave now, but it wouldn't be any easier than if he left later. That is, if he left after finding Nick Blanco.

Bridger looked down the hall. Then he looked at the room number that said 310. Kept his eyes on that for a moment, then looked at the rooms on either side of 310. He turned and looked at the room directly across. Room 311.

He went back to the stairs. He walked, quietly, up to the next floor. Stopped and listened for sounds. He didn't hear anything so he kept going. On the fifth floor he stopped again.

Stopped and listened . . .

Voices. Coming from the next floor up. Or maybe the one above that. Murmurs that were not too distinct, but he listened harder and notes seemed to fall into place. Two men conversing, one of them saying Terrell Owens was a selfish nigger and he could go fuck himself. The other one, being correct, responding, yeah, but McNabb, he's okay and you shouldn't assume they all weren't team players. Then both of them agreeing that the union lawyer and Owens's agent were both pieces of shit.

Bridger edged to the doorway to the hall, cracked it open. Widened the crack as quietly as he could until he could slip through it.

He was on the fifth floor now, the voices cut off. He looked at the numbers on the doors again and found 510 and 511. He remembered that the fire escape was on the odd side, the 511 side. At first, he wanted it to be the other way around and he tried to think if it had been and he was just disori-

310

ented. But he knew it wasn't and he knew from his earlier check that there was only one fire escape. He stood in the hallway and thought it out and decided maybe it wasn't too bad this way. He went to room 503 and jimmied the door open and slipped in.

There was no one in the room. Which didn't surprise him. He went to the window and looked down. A couple of guys in the back alley, smoking cigarettes. Bridger looked to his right and saw the fire escape was about two rooms down. He went back to the hall.

He walked down the hall to room 507 and went in to that one. He walked to the window and opened it by degrees. When it was opened at first, he heard city traffic in the distance and smelled the mixture of butane and crude from the Sunoco refinery. He looked down and saw the same men he had seen before. They had not gone any-where and now he could hear their voices too. He thought about it briefly . . . they had not looked up yet and there was no point in staring at them until they did. He stepped out onto the fire escape and began his ascent.

He was not a rooftop sort of guy. Maggie had once kidded him, asking if he was like Cary Grant in that movie with Grace Kelly.

Jumping around rooftops in black clothing, flexing his hands as he crouched. No, Bridger had said, that guy had worked in the circus before becoming a thief. You had to be in shape, that was a given, but you didn't need to be an acrobat. If you were jumping from one building to another it was only a matter of time before the chasm would be too wide and you would plummet to your death. Or, get lit up like a Christmas tree by a police helicopter's spotlight before taking a sniper's bullet in the back, the eager cop having already told himself that he could have sworn he saw the flash of a weapon.

Bridger got to the eighth floor without someone shining a flashlight on him or unloading weapons. He got the window open and let himself in. Once in, he thought about shutting the window, but figured he shouldn't press his luck.

Room 807, he thought. *You're in room 807.*

He moved to his left and put his ear against the door. He listened for voices or a radio or anything that would tell him that there were men in the next room. He counted to sixty, then did it again. He opened the first door and pressed his ear against the second one. Still, no sound.

After that, he began the process of picking

the lock and getting the second door open. He worked it for a while, being patient and sure. Soon, he felt it loosen. He opened it a crack and looked inside. Saw nothing.

He stepped in.

There was no one there. He looked out the window. He didn't know what he expected to see out there. Vampires floating or a stray helicopter. It didn't make sense to look, but you did anyway. Nothing out there but the dingy part of the city and the lights and the smoke of the refinery beyond.

And then he heard men talking.

In the next room.

Room 811.

So his instinct had been right. Blanco had men posted in the room across the hall.

But they weren't talking. They were . . . whispering. Hiding. Keeping their voices low until the chump came down the hall and tried to go into the room across from them. Then . . . what? Step out into the hall and blow his head off with a shotgun? Or do it the old-fashioned way, with a .22 pistol placed right against the back of the head and pull the trigger five or six times, better to be safe than sorry.

Bridger removed the .45 from his pocket and a silencer from his other pocket. He screwed the silencer into the barrel of the gun. When it was tight, but not too tight, he moved to the next set of double doors. He raised one hand and slowly twisted the knob to unlock the door. Slowly, he pulled the door open, revealing the second door.

He could not pick the lock on the next one. They would hear the scratches and probably shoot him through the door. He wished it could be otherwise, but it couldn't be.

He stepped back and balanced himself and then kicked the door in with all he had.

Things moved quickly. One of the men inside already had a shotgun in his hands and he was starting to level it and Bridger shot him twice in the chest and the man was down.

The second man had stepped back in fright and was reaching for a gun in his belt and Bridger said, "Ahh," like you would say to a dog that was misbehaving. And the guy put his hands above his head.

Bridger stepped over to him and took the gun out of the man's waistband and pushed him down onto the bed.

"Keep your hands on your head," Bridger said.

Bridger took the shotgun away from the man on the ground, who was dead now. He held it in his other hand as he looked at the man who was sitting on the bed.

Bridger said, "How much you getting paid for this?"

"Not enough."

Bridger smiled. "Yeah, that's what I'd say. Tell me who else is on this floor and you get to go home tonight."

"I —" He was hesitating.

"Or," Bridger said, gesturing to the corpse, "you can go with him."

"It's Maddox across the hall. He's alone in there. They've got guys in both stairwells, though. You'll never get out of here."

"Maddox? Claude Maddox?"

"Yeah."

"He's working for Blanco?"

"Yeah," the guy said. "For a while now."

Claude Maddox? Bridger thought. He was out of Pittsburgh. Grew up in one of those dingy mountain towns. Liked to hunt a lot. How long had he been in Philly?

Bridger said, "What about Nick?"

"What about him?"

"Where is he?"

"He's not here."

Bridger raised his gun arm.

"I swear, man. He's not fucking here."

Bridger sighed. *Shit.* He wasn't surprised, but he had hoped Blanco would be here. Bridger said, "Turn around."

"Hey, I've got a kid —"

"Just turn around," Bridger said. "You're going home."

The guy turned around and Bridger hit him behind his right ear with the .45. He slumped over.

Later, Bridger thought. *You'll go home later.*

FORTY-ONE

When he got to the room, Maddox had arranged the furniture so that it was almost situated like an office. He had taken the night table from next to the bed and placed it so that it was about six feet in front of the door. Then he had placed the attaché case on top, so that the first thing you would see when you walked in was the table with the black case on it.

The attaché case was closed, its latches facing the door. It would draw attention from the entrant right away and he would think, *hey, there it is* and tell himself there was money inside.

There was money inside too. About three or four hundred dollars in loose bills, lying on top of newspapers that had been spray painted green. Nothing too fancy, but it would hold your attention for a couple of seconds, sustain the illusion for that long and that would be all that Maddox would need.

The other thing that Maddox had done was moved the desk away from the wall and set it so that it faced the night table and the door behind it. He would be sitting behind the desk when, or if, Bridger came through that door. The drawer on his left was open and sitting in the drawer was a long-barreled .44 revolver. Crude and too loud for stealthy work, but it never jammed and it would leave a hole the size of an apple through a man's chest.

Maddox had walked around the room and looked at his arrangement from different angles and positions. From the door, he could not even tell if the desk drawer was open, let alone if there was a gun in there. And the sight of the attaché case and its promise of easy money was a pleasant distraction even to him. And he *knew* its contents were worthless. People like their illusions.

The final prop was the sports page of the *Philadelphia Inquirer* spread open on the desk. It would lead the man to believe that Maddox was a chop. Not taking the job too seriously, flipping through the sports page to kill time. Again, not the sort of illusion that would sustain for a long time, but he wouldn't need long. He only needed a few seconds.

He was rattled when he heard the car alarm. But then it stopped and one of the men radioed him and told him they hadn't seen anything. And after that, he told himself that maybe Bridger was in the building and maybe he wasn't. If he was, fine. He was the same man that Maddox had got the jump on and thrown down a flight of stairs. It gave him a confidence about the man that he felt he'd earned.

Maddox finished the *USA Today* crossword puzzle and set it on the corner of the desk. After that, he started on the *New York Times* crossword, in ink as usual. He was starting to get a handle on the running theme of the long ones that went all the way across when he heard the noise across the hall.

He stopped, cocked his head.

It was not loud. No gunfire that he could hear. No shout or scream. A sort of muffled sound.

He kept still, listening for something. Anything.

But nothing.

He put his pen down and picked up the revolver and walked to the door. He stood in front of the door for a moment, then slowly turned the knob and opened it.

Bridger was standing in the open doorway across the hall, a gun in his right hand, pointed toward the ground, in almost the same pose as Maddox.

How long they exchanged a glance, neither one could know. A second? A half-second? Maybe less.

And then Claude Maddox raised the .44 and squeezed the trigger. Hard, because it had not been cocked and it had about a four-pound pull and it may have been that that saved the other man's life.

A .44 revolver sounds like a small cannon, particularly when it is fired in an enclosed area. It boomed out once, twice, echoing off the dingy walls of the hotel hallway, Bridger stepping to his right as the shots went past him, Maddox staying where he was for the first two shots, then moving forward as he kept pulling the trigger and Bridger was crouched now, on his knees and out of view, and he had to put his pistol in his left hand so that only his hand and arm would be exposed and he put his head out just enough to see the man coming close and he fired four times.

Two of the shots caught Maddox in his midsection, the third punching him in his chest and he fell back and the fourth shot went over his shoulder and the gun flipped out of his hand and he was on his back, the life coming out of him.

He was aware of the light down the hall, fading in and out, his vision blurring. Aware of Bridger stepping out, moving quickly, getting near the .44 and throwing it aside. Which didn't make any difference now, he didn't have the strength to move, yet alone scramble after the pistol. There was the ceiling and the man's head and shoulders and not much else in his world at this moment.

The man saying something now . . .

What?

Bridger said, "Was it you? Was it you at the man's house?"

Not saying the man's name. Hannon. Judge Joe Hannon. Knowing his name made little difference now.

"Was it?" Bridger said.

Maddox managed to lift his head, his neck muscles doing all the work. He formed a smile. "Yeah," he said. "How's your head?" He laughed. Then his laugh became a cough and he put his head back down. He stopped coughing. His eyes fluttered for a moment, then remained open. He was dead.

Bridger heard a sound to his right. Christ, the elevator. Coming into place now as the doors opened and three guys came running out, all of them armed.

Bridger ran back into the room and picked up the shotgun. Racked the slide and stepped back out and shot one of them in the leg while he was still running. The man screamed and went down, a good part of his thigh gone now. Bridger's second shot hit the wall, missing the other two guys but splattering plaster on them and getting them to run back the other way. He held his fire, then dodged back into the room.

Bridger waited a moment before peering back out. The man was on the ground, crying and yelling and rolling about, the other two gone. Bridger looked down the hall and saw a door on the other side was open. The other two had gone in there.

He called out to them.

"Hey. I didn't come here for you. Stay out of this and you get to go home. Step out and you die."

There was no response.

Bridger said, "Now close that door."

A few seconds passed by. Then the door was pushed shut.

Bridger stepped back into the room and closed the door behind him. He stuck a chair up underneath the doorknob and moved back to the double doors on the side. He made his way back to the room with the fire escape. He still had the shotgun. He debated it for a moment and decided he would be better off without it now. He hid it in a closet, then stepped out onto the fire escape.

There was a one-story carport across the alley from the hotel. But Bridger saw that the alley was probably more of a driveway because there was chain link fence at the end at the front of the hotel and a brick wall at the other. He had seen it before but now he was seeing it in a different way. The good news was the men that had been more or less in the middle of the drive before were now standing by the chain link fence. Maybe because they had been told he would probably try to blast his way out of the front. Two men, looking out front, not behind them.

Bridger got down to the second story and saw that there were two vehicles in the carport. A Ford Taurus and a Chevy pick-up truck. He dropped to the ground and darted across the drive into the carport.

The Chevy truck was parked so that its front faced out. It was an older model, late eighties. And Bridger had noticed its antenna. He snapped the antenna off and bent it into a U-shape. Then he stuck it down between the window and the door. It was dark, and darker in the shadows of the carport, so he had to work by feel more than sight. It took him over a minute to find the lock and pull the bent antenna up on it.

And then the door was unlocked.

Bridger got into the truck. He left the door open. He bent down and pulled the ignition wires from the steering column. He wrapped two of them together. He paused then and thought it out. When the truck started, the men at the fence would hear it. He would have to move quickly after that because there was only one way out.

With that in mind, he touched the third wire to the hot wire. It kicked the starter and the engine turned over. Bridger shut the door and put the gearshift in drive. Hit the gas and pulled out and turned right. Men were coming toward him, curious and surprised at first, but guns in hand, which they were starting to raise . . .

Bridger flipped on the headlights, then brighted them and floored the accelerator. One of the guys got a shot off, which thwacked through the passenger side of the windshield, but Bridger kept going and the men jumped to either side of the drive, parting for him as the fence came into view and Bridger kept the accelerator to the floor, the engine roaring now.

The Chevy truck bashed the fence open

and Bridger cranked the wheel to the right again, away from the hotel. He was conscious of startled faces, more men at the front of the hotel, shouting and shots cracked out, one of which he heard pinging off the tailgate. And then the truck was down the road and gone.

FORTY-TWO

Lacey had told him before, "It's not called the Philadelphia Philharmonic. There's no such thing as the Philadelphia Philharmonic. It's the Philadelphia Orchestra."

Nick Blanco didn't see the big deal. Philharmonic, orchestra . . . who gives a shit? But his wife seemed to put stock in things like that.

On this night, they were in the Verizon Hall of the Kimmel Center watching the orchestra perform Beethoven's Seventh Symphony. Nick thought it was okay. Stirring, almost. The conductor looked like one of those bad guys in old James Bond films and he was moving his arms with feeling, more and more, as the piece gathered steam and marched through its crescendo. Lacey had told him that Beethoven had written it to inspire the Austrians to win the Battle of Waterloo. Nick nodded his head, being thoughtful. Before the intermission, they had some lady from Scotland who didn't wear any shoes and did nothing but bong on a big set of drums. It bored the shit out of Nick, and he wondered if that part would go past midnight. Finally, intermission came and he and Lacey went out to the lobby and drank wine while Lacey pointed out people who were members of the Philadelphia Orchestra Association. She introduced him to a few people she seemed to know and he didn't . . . one or two of them looking nervous, knowing who he was and what he did. Though Lacey didn't seem to notice.

That was one of the things he valued about Lacey. Most of the time, he valued it. She didn't seem to notice things like people being put off by the fact that her husband was a gangster. She never gave him heat about what he did. Indeed, she never even asked about it. It was as if it didn't exist. She had constructed for herself a world of nice things and pretty people.

To help maintain this illusion, Nick Blanco had to do things like this with her. He had to go to symphonies. He had to sit through *Cats*. Once, he even had to go to New York to watch some play where a bunch of women got on stage and talked about their pussies. Afterward, he told Lacey he didn't see the point of it. She pointed out to him that one of the women used to be married to the mayor. Like that made a fuck.

It was almost eleven forty-five when they wrapped up Beethoven's Seventh and they turned up the lights for good. The valet brought the Cadillac around and Nick tipped him twenty bucks.

Lacey said, "Do you want to stop by the Polo Club for a drink?"

"No," Nick said. "I'm expecting a call."

Lacey didn't ask from whom. She knew she would be in bed while he took the call in another room. Probably his office downstairs. Or the kitchen. Sometimes he would gesture with his head after picking up the phone, letting her know she needed to leave the room.

When they got home, she turned to him in the living room and said, "I'll be upstairs." Telling him she was in the mood for it. She usually was after one of those symphonies.

Nick watched her remove her earrings.

"I won't be long," he said.

He turned on the little television in the kitchen to watch the local news. They were showing highlights of the Sixers games, the player from the visiting team hitting nine treys against them tonight. Nick went to the refrigerator and took out a bottle of beer and stood at the counter.

The sports anchor saying the Sixers couldn't get a break tonight.

Nick looked at the telephone hanging on the wall. Stared at it for a few moments.

He walked over to the drawers by the counter. Opened one.

"It isn't in there," Bridger said.

He didn't turn around at first. Didn't even turn his head. He looked down in the drawer and saw that the gun he usually kept there had been removed. He smiled and then gave a short laugh. "Ah, fuck. I should have known." Then he turned around.

Bridger was holding a .45 with a silencer attached to the barrel.

Nick's hands were on the counter behind him.

Nick said, "I guess you searched the place pretty well."

"Just the kitchen. I didn't have time to search the rest of the house."

"You just hoped I'd come in here?"

"You're waiting for a call, aren't you?"

"Yeah, I was. I guess I'm not going to get one, huh?"

Bridger said, "Not from Maddox."

Nick Blanco slowly nodded his head. "Well," he said, "I guess you can kill me too. But the Tessas have long arms. I'd say it isn't worth it."

"Yeah? Was this whole thing their idea or yours?"

Nick Blanco didn't say anything. Or he waited too long to respond.

"Yeah," Bridger said, "that's what I thought."

Nick said, "Look, man, I don't even know you. Can't you see that this wasn't a personal thing? You steal, you think you're doing it *to* them? We needed someone to take the fall and you fit the bill. Nothing more to it than that."

"Hmmm."

"You want money, I'll give you money."

"We're past that."

"We're past? — Christ. You mean this is about Maggie? Buddy, I knew her before you did. She's the one that brought you into this. If she knew you were doing this, she'd be fucking laughing at you right now."

Bridger shrugged. "Yeah, maybe she would. But that's not really the point."

"You don't —"

It was brief, but Bridger caught it. Caught the man's eyes shift to his left, Bridger's right, and as Bridger turned to his right to see what it was, he heard Blanco say, "Shoot him." And the woman raised the gun and

330

Bridger jumped toward her, rushing her, knowing in that brief millisecond that he couldn't bring himself to shoot her, but she was close enough to rush and Bridger was a half step to her when she pulled the trigger and he felt it hit his leg before he collided with her and they both went down.

He was fogged with pain, red and white, and he saw Blanco coming into view, coming quickly, bending down to the ground to pick up Lacey's gun, picking it up now and turning as Bridger concentrated and lifted his gun and fired three times and Blanco went down, the third shot catching him in the chest.

Bridger went over to him on hands and knees and batted the revolver across the kitchen floor. He looked at the woman. She was unconscious, her head having hit the floor when she fell. She was alive, though.

Bridger brought himself to his knees and looked at Nick. He got over to him and felt for a pulse on his neck. There was none.

With effort, he got to his feet. He walked to the sink and took a dish towel from the rack and wrapped it around his leg. The bullet had gone through, but had missed the vein; he would not bleed out.

He turned around and surveyed the scene. Blanco dead, the woman alive. The woman had seen him. He could kill her and take that worry off his plate. Kill the mobster's wife. She would have killed him if she'd been quicker. Kill her and be done with it.

In the distance, he heard a siren.

And the woman was still there. Still unconscious. And for some reason, she made him think of Claire. The judge's wife. Thought of her and knew he couldn't do it.

The sirens were drawing closer.

Bridger went over to Nick Blanco. He squatted next to Blanco and took Claire Laval's diamond earrings out of his pocket. They were still in the tissue. He placed the earrings in Blanco's hand and squeezed the hand shut, covering them. Then, using the tissue, he took them back out and put them in Blanco's jacket pocket.

He stood up and looked over to see Blanco's overcoat hanging over a kitchen chair. He took it as a sign of luck. A long black coat. He put it on and saw that it covered the part of his leg that was wrapped in a towel, staining red now. He would be limping, for a few days anyway, but the coat would hide the wound for tonight.

He went out the back door and was in the neighbor's yard when the first police car pulled into the front drive.

He walked for three quarters of a mile

before he found a bus. He got on and took a seat near the back.

FORTY-THREE

Trooper Lytle introduced her to a city detective and a black FBI agent. Trooper Pierce was there too. Men sitting at her kitchen table, some of them sipping coffee she had made for them. Taking turns looking at each other to see which one of them would ask the next question.

They asked her a lot of questions about Joe and his connections to the Tessas. She was no more helpful than she had been before, and she knew it. But she was patient and didn't seem to be in any hurry.

Finally, the Philadelphia detective, who earlier had said his name was Morrow, said, "I want to show you something." He took out an evidence bag. It was clear and it had a yellow evidence tag on it.

Claire looked through the plastic baggie and her heart seemed to stop for a moment.

Lt. Morrow said, "Are these yours?"

Claire reached over and slid the baggie

toward her. "Yes," she said. "They've been missing for a while. Where did you find these?"

"They were in Nick Blanco's pocket," Morrow said. "We figured they might belong to his wife. But she said they didn't."

Lytle said, "Why didn't you report that, Claire? Why didn't you report that they were missing?"

"I . . . didn't think about it, I guess." She paused, remembering the conversation in the car, slipping the earrings into his pocket in the dark. "With all that was going on."

"Well," Morrow said. "That's certainly understandable."

"It was a hunch we had," the black agent said. "And we wanted to check it out. Turns out we were right."

Claire stared into her coffee cup for a moment. The chance meeting in the coffee shop, the questioning in the cabin, the time they had in the hotel room . . . he had not called her to tell her he was all right. He would not do that, she knew.

Claire said, "I'm sorry, sir. I've forgotten your name."

"Agent Roarke. Adam Roarke."

"Mister Roarke," Claire said, "did Mrs. Blanco say who — who killed her husband?"

Agent Roarke turned to Morrow and

335

Morrow gave him a shrug. Why not tell her?

Roarke said, "She did not. We believe it was someone from the Tessa Family. And we believe she knows that. That's why she's not talking."

Morrow said, "Blanco had become a liability to them."

Claire looked directly at Morrow and then at Roarke. She shook her head then, almost shuddered. "It's all so violent," she said.

"Yes, it is," Morrow said. "But for you, it's over now." He smiled at her. "Okay?"

Claire said, "Okay."

ABOUT THE AUTHOR

James Patrick Hunt was born in Surrey, England, in 1964. He graduated from Parks College of Saint Louis University with a degree in aerospace engineering in 1986 and from Marquette University Law School in 1992. He resides in Tulsa, Oklahoma, where he writes and practices law. He is the author of *Maitland, Maitland Under Siege, Before They Make You Run, The Betrayers, Goodbye Sister Disco, The Assailant, Maitland's Reply,* and *The Silent Places.*